N
W
E
S
CANADA
GUELPH
HONG KONG
PHILIPPINES
PALAWAN
SOUTH CHINA SEA
EL NIDO
MALIPAYON COVE
PALAWAN
SULU SEA

DJ MacDonald

Book One: A Tale of a Malipayon Warrior

CORIE LARAYA-COUTTS
HANNE LORE KOEHLER

iUniverse, Inc.
New York Bloomington

iUniverse books may be ordered through booksellers or by contacting:

iUniverse
1663 Liberty Drive
Bloomington, IN 47403
www.iuniverse.com
1-800-Authors (1-800-288-4677)

ISBN: 978-1-4502-1346-2 (sc)
ISBN: 978-1-4502-1344-8 (hc)
ISBN: 978-1-4502-1345-5 (ebook)

Library of Congress Control Number: 2010902209

Printed in the United States of America

iUniverse rev. date: 03/18/2010

For my late father, Narciso Laraya Sr., who
taught me to how to dream and fly;

and

for my husband, Rod, my mentor, my teacher, my
best friend, who gave me wings so that I could fly.

"All our dreams can come true if we have the courage to pursue them."

Walt Disney

"Imagination will often carry us to worlds that never were; but without it, we go nowhere."

Carl Sagan

Contents

Acknowledgments

My journey in writing this book has been very special. It has opened the door for me to revisit my cultural background as a Filipino who was raised by tenant farmer parents in the southern part of Mindanao, Philippines.

This book would not have materialized without the help of my dear friend Hanne Lore Koehler. To Bill and Monica McConkey and their family, and Anuppa Calekal-Ruton, who endured a few weeks of reading and gave me insightful criticism: a heartfelt thank you.

I thank the many people who have become part of me for a great experience and memories. The list includes: the late Jose Perez and his family; the Sotelo family; Mr. Benigno Sobrevega and his family; Ken and Rogie Smith and family; Dr. and Mrs. Maher Al-Basha and family; Simon and Lovina Ng; and Mr. and Mrs. S. Asaad.

Thanks to my adopted country, Canada, for the opportunity to explore my dreams. To the people and city of Guelph, Ontario: every time I witness the twin towers of the magnificent Our Lady Immaculate Church, I am truly inspired.

To the residents of Palawan, and to my brother and sisters of Jolo, Sulu: your islands are truly a "heaven on earth."

Thanks to my hometown, Norala, South Cotabato, that raised me to become who I am today. To the B'laan and T'boli clan of South Cotabato, the traditions and culture that you hold to this day humble me deeply, and I recognize the dedication and hardship of every Filipino Overseas Worker. You are all part of this exciting passage too.

Thanks to all of our friends who have supported and had faith in me, and to Andrew Halsall of Riverside Band for allowing me to use their name in this book.

Finally, thanks to my family who challenged, inspired, and gave me strength. No words can express how special you are to me. I love you all: my mother Fresca Laraya, my four brothers and seven sisters, nieces and nephews; my stepchildren Leigh Ann and Rob Pitre, Sherri, Tracy, and Brad; and to my two precious grandchildren, Joshua and Emma Pitre.

— 1 —

DJ's Vivid Visions

The tide was low. Fourteen-year-old DJ was alone inside a gazebo up on a little hill at the end of a sandbar. The gazebo was made of solid wrought-iron bars that had been twisted and hammered into the most complex shapes anyone could imagine. DJ saw how the delicate ornamental design masked the strength of the material and realized that things are not always what they seem. A tangle of thorny vines was intertwined with the intricate structure covering it with spectacular blooms of different colors—magenta, gold, orange, and white—as if nature had approved of this artistic marvel.

As he wondered who could have built such a masterpiece, DJ spotted two silhouettes walking toward him on the beach. He squinted against the brilliant colors of the setting sun and as the figures drew closer, he realized they were his grandfather and grandmother.

"Grandpa, Lola, over here!" he called.

The warm gentle ocean waves were lapping at their feet as they smiled and waved at him. Then, as they were about to reach the end of the s-shaped sandbar at the foot of the hill, it began to writhe and flail from side-to-side. In a blink, the idyllic south sea scene turned morbid. The sky grew ominous with deep purple clouds. Suddenly, an enormous fire-breathing snake emerged from the sand beneath his grandparents.

DJ wanted to run to their rescue but his feet froze in place. His chest was pounding and aching with terror, but all he could do was watch as his grandparents were flung into the ocean and then vanished. The snake began to slither toward him. Stunned and bewildered, he could not shout or move…

"Acting up again, dude?" The sound of Hanna's loud voice interrupted the terror. "Hey DJ, you're not seeing those things again, are you?" she asked as she looked into his glazed eyes. She was referring to the mysterious images that had been plaguing DJ for nearly a year.

"Ah-hmm, what did you say?" asked DJ, still dazed and confused by his vivid vision. His eyes began to refocus on reality. His dog, Kibbles, raised his paw to DJ's knee and seemed to let out a little understanding whine.

"Forget it. I will go and use my computer then." Hanna headed to the bedroom door.

"No, no… I'm fine," he said as he turned back to his laptop. He dismissed the vision for his sister's sake and hoped she would stay. Thirteen-year-old Hanna sensed that he needed her company as a distraction from another episode, so she returned to the extra chair at his desk. They continued where they had left off surfing the Net for information about the Philippines, but DJ could not get the vision out of his mind.

DJ and Hanna MacDonald had been told earlier that evening by their mom and dad that the family was going on a trip to the Philippines for a family reunion. Excited by the prospect of visiting a distant country, the home of their ancestors on their mom's side of the family, they had decided to research the Philippines on the Internet. They were surprised to learn from their Web search that this small country had over seven thousand islands and that four thousand of them were inhabited by only eighty-two tribes. A website photo of a sunset on one of the islands' beaches had triggered DJ's latest vision.

"Wow, this is amazing!" Hanna was in awe as they learned more about their mother Laura's culture, to which they had not paid too much attention before; on the other hand, they had not paid too much attention to their father's Scottish culture, either.

DJ MacDonald was a smart, normal student at St. James Catholic High School in Guelph, Ontario. Like many Canadian boys at age fourteen, his life revolved around sports, especially hockey. His tanned complexion and black hair had obviously developed from his mom's Filipino genes, but his stunning blue eyes, good humor, athleticism, and his six-foot stature had been passed to him from his father Alex's Scottish ancestry.

Hannah also had a tanned complexion with long flowing black hair. She was slim, energetic, out-going, and already a little taller than her mother. Hanna's interests lay in music and boys. With two of her friends from school, she had formed a rock band called "The Girlfriends" that had been well accepted by the kids at school.

It had become a tradition for their mother's family to organize a family reunion every four years. Laura was the oldest of twelve siblings. She had nine sisters and two brothers. All were married now with families of their own and lived in different countries all over the world. Only the youngest son, Laura's brother, Godfrey, and his wife still lived with their parents. It is a Filipino tradition that parents look after their children when they are young and children look after their parents when they are old. Filipinos honor this tradition to this day.

Four years earlier, the family had met in Germany at the home of Laura's sister, Carmelita, and her husband, Fritz Schroeder. Carmelita was a pharmacist and Fritz, who was born in Germany, was an anesthesiologist. The Schroeders lived in Cologne and had a son named Hans who was just a few months younger than DJ. They also had a daughter, Kirsten, who was about the same age as Hanna. It was a great reunion.

Laura's parents had planned to host the next reunion coming up in March at their farm in Socsargen on the island of Mindanao; however, there was a sudden change to the plans and the venue of the gathering had been moved to another island called El Nido, Palawan. Only the adults in the family knew the reasons for this change because in this family, children never interfered in adult decisions and this was understood.

Thoughts of the horrifying images of his vision lingered in DJ's mind as they used Google Earth to find their destination. El Nido was located southwest of Manila, the country's capital city. Locals and tourists called it "heaven on earth." It had forty-five islands or islets; each one had its own geological formations, its own wildlife, and its own fascinating history.

Neither DJ, Hanna, nor their parents had ever been to the island that Grandpa owned. They knew that he had inherited an island somewhere way back when, but it had never been discussed further in the family. No one had been interested at all until recently, when DJ overheard his mom talking to one of her sisters about a cottage that their parents were building on an island. Although Laura loved her home in Canada, she missed her family and like all of her siblings, she looked forward to the family reunions.

DJ and Hanna also looked forward with anticipation and excitement to see their grandparents and cousins again and especially to see the mysterious island. The four months until their trip seemed like a long time to wait. Hanna yawned and headed for DJ's door.

"I'm beat," she said, "and I have band practice before class in the morning." Then she added as she walked out, "I wonder what kind of wildlife lives on the island—probably tigers or wild boars and snakes!"

"Snakes," DJ groaned, recalling his latest frightening vision. He lay down on his bed, his feet widely spread touching the floor, "and they probably breathe fire, too!" he said sarcastically to himself. DJ tried to find a comfortable position and concentrated on thinking about other things so that he could fall asleep, but the vision kept overpowering his thoughts. Since DJ's nightmares began, Kibbles seemed to want to comfort him and remained by his side at night, curled up in his bed on the floor beside DJ's bed.

DJ's mind wandered to the disturbing dream he had had the week before in which an enormous ogre with the head of a snake and a scale-covered human-shaped body was wielding a sword, and hissing as it stood guard over a prisoner. The prisoner was an odd-looking creature with the head and wings of an eagle and the body of a water buffalo. It seemed to be very weak and dying. It appeared to be reaching out to DJ for help. The entire scene took place under the ocean and seemed so real and detailed that he could almost touch the rock columns that confined the prisoner. DJ had awoken from the nightmare gasping for air as if he were about to drown. His mom and dad had come running into his room to see if he was all right. He recalled being drenched. Had it been from sweat or seawater?

His parents were worried, especially his mom. She realized that DJ was tormented by disturbing daytime visions as well as night terrors, in which he seemed to be fighting an unseen battle. She had tried to persuade him to see a specialist or a professional that dealt with this kind of issue, but DJ had refused vigorously.

Why was he having such vivid visions of what seemed to be another world? How could he stop the night terrors that crept into and prevailed over his normal dreams? Where were these strange places and who were these outrageous creatures in his dreams? He stared at the ceiling and after what seemed like hours, he finally fell asleep.

— 2 —

Halloween Spirit

This year, Halloween fell on Friday and a party was organized at St. James High School for all the students. Costumes were compulsory for those who chose to attend. Most kids were excited but not DJ. After much coaxing from his friend, Nick, however, at the last minute DJ reluctantly agreed to go to the party. With his mom's help, they searched the house for available materials and improvised a costume for him to wear.

A couple of weeks had passed without any terrible visions and DJ hoped that was the last of them.

Late that afternoon, the brisk breeze from the north was cold and damp. Dried maple and birch leaves that covered the yard hissed and swirled in gusts. Daylight hours were shorter now and darkness came early. A neighbor had given them a couple of pumpkins from his vegetable garden and DJ and his dad had carved them with wicked eyes a few nights earlier. With glowing candles flickering from inside the pumpkins, they looked spooky sitting on the hay bale and chrysanthemum display beside the front door.

The MacDonalds lived in an average-sized, renovated, thirty-year-old home. It was situated on a hill on Base Line Road overlooking Guelph Lake and a golf course just outside the small city of Guelph, Ontario. Because they lived out in the country, where fields and stands of trees separated neighbors, only a handful of young neighborhood ghosts and goblins ever came trick-or-treating. They were always accompanied by their parents. Since Laura, a pediatrician, had been there when the children were born, she always filled Halloween bags with special treats for them. The younger kids could not stay up too late, so trick-or-treat visits were brief and ended by 7:30 p.m.

Hanna looked stunning. With sparkling sequins and flowing feathers, her black witch costume was anything but traditional. Since she was going to perform with The Girlfriends at the Halloween party that evening during the disc jockey's break, she and her friends had rented their special costumes a week earlier and, unlike DJ, she was excited and enthusiastic to go to the party.

Even DJ looked cool. He was dressed like a Goth in a black cloak with a hood and a wooden crucifix necklace painted in black. He wore black gloves and a pair of old army boots that actually fit. His face was painted white with costume makeup. He had black lips and a big raw red scar on his forehead. The blood that dripped to his cheek looked real.

Around 8:30 in the evening, Alex drove a still-reluctant DJ and a nervous Hanna with her electric guitar to the school in town. Kids wearing all sorts of grotesque costumes were swarming the entrance door of St. James. A load of noisy teens burst out of a minivan.

"Have fun, guys! Text me when you're ready—no later than midnight," said Alex.

"Thanks for the ride, Dad," said Hanna as she hurried out of the car to her waiting friends. They gushed over each other's costumes and went inside to set up their instruments.

DJ met a few classmates that were standing by, teasing and commenting on each other's costumes.

"Whew! You look awesome, man," said the kid in a vampire costume.

"Do you know if Nick is here yet?" DJ asked.

"I saw him heading in that direction." The vampire pointed toward the church. DJ knew that some kids go to the mall beside the church for cigarettes and coffee but that was out of character for Nick. DJ thought the vampire must be mistaken and went inside.

He decided to use the men's room first and sent Nick a text message: "Where d hell are u? I'm in the hall."

There was nobody inside the men's room. He stood looking into the mirror. The face of an old man with wrinkled and gloomy eyes was looking back at him. DJ blinked a few times in hopes that the image would go away. The painted blood on his forehead began to trickle down his face. He touched it. It was real blood! Freaked out, he ran out of the washroom and almost knocked down someone coming in the door.

"Hey, what's with you? Retard," said an angry kid.

DJ walked quickly until he reached the scene of the party in the huge triple gym. Kids were dancing to the beat of Riverside's version of "The Best is Yet to Come." He decided to walk through the gym to look for Nick but had no luck. He checked his cell phone for a reply from Nick, but there was none.

He was a little upset. This was Nick's idea. Where was he? His anger changed to concern when he realized that it was unlike Nick not to show up as planned. He started to feel anxious. Worried about his best friend, he decided to go and look for him at the nearby mall beyond the church.

At that time of the night, the streets were still busy. Older kids, revelers, were giggling over the amount of treats they had collected. He took a piece of chewing gum from his pocket and popped it into his mouth.

DJ could see the mall in the distance past Our Lady Immaculate Church, which overlooked the MacDonnell Street hill below. He reached into his pocket for his iPod Nano, stuck one of the earphones in his left ear and listened to a rap by The Black-Eyed Peas as he walked briskly.

As he neared the church an old man, who seemed to appear from out of nowhere, asked DJ if he knew a short cut into the church, explaining that he felt too weak to walk all the way around to the front doors of the huge building.

"It's cold tonight, eh?" said the old man. DJ removed his earphones.

"Yeah, winter is coming, I'm afraid," DJ responded as he pointed out a nearby entrance. The old man thanked him and stumbled as he shuffled away. DJ realized he was holding a white cane. He walked over to him and said, "I'll take you."

As DJ slowly led the elder to the nearby entrance, a thick fog suddenly enveloped them. The old man distracted him with questions, and when DJ looked up, he could not see the door to the church. He could see only a dim light above the door that glowed through the fog.

The man silently followed him while holding on to DJ's arm. The way to the entrance door seemed endless. The light appeared to get further away the nearer they got. DJ was suddenly unsure of where he was.

Embarrassed, he murmured, "I know it's somewhere here. We just used it yesterday."

When he turned to apologize to the old man, he saw that the man was wearing the same Goth costume as his. DJ could not see his face because the hood of his cloak was pulled down over his head and the fog was so thick. An eerie feeling gripped the pit of his stomach. Was this another vision? Was this the old man from the mirror at school?

DJ picked up the pace. His heart was pounding in his chest. Surprisingly, the old man kept up. They walked in silence among the weather-worn remnants of headstones of the centuries-old cemetery on the left side of the church. Suddenly, they stood in front of the entrance to the church. DJ breathed a sigh of relief as he opened the door and led the old man inside into the light. The huge solid oak door creaked closed behind them.

"Here we are," said DJ and as he turned to leave, he felt the weight of the old man's powerful hand on his shoulder, but he could not see it. DJ froze. He was unable to move his feet.

"Who are you? What do you want from me?" DJ demanded but the quiver in his voice betrayed his fear. The entrance hall was well lit but still no face was visible.

The sides of the cloak worn by the metaphysical being lifted as though it had raised both arms wide and he said, "I have an important message for you. You are called for a very special mission and you will require something to assist you," said the haunting voice.

"Who are you to tell me that? I want to go home now!" DJ exclaimed.

"It is not important who I am. It is you who is important. You have a big task to accomplish. I am a good spirit here to aid you. Have no fear. Look around you," said the apparition.

DJ hesitantly shifted his gaze from the apparition to his surroundings and recognized the church library. Books filled the shelves from floor to ceiling. DJ had been there many times. His family attended Our Lady Immaculate Church regularly, but DJ had no recollection of how he had gotten from the church entrance door to the library that day.

"You have been wondering about the source of your visions and why they are happening. Here you will find the beginning of all the answers you seek," said the spirit.

DJ was stunned that the spirit knew about his visions. He had not told anyone for fear that he would be ridiculed. Only his mom, dad, and Hanna knew because they had witnessed many frightening episodes when DJ seemed to be in another world. Was it possible that this spirit could really help him? DJ listened as the supernatural being continued.

"In these four pillars, there are invisible drawers. Find one and there will be a message for you," said the good spirit.

DJ warily kept one eye on the spirit as he approached the pillars.

"Maybe this is for real—maybe not. What can it hurt if I play along?" he said to himself.

As a test of the spirit's sincerity, he chose a spot near the top of the third pillar and felt his body levitate to it. As he reached out to the pillar, a drawer that had been invisible opened. Inside was a small, worn, dusty book about the size of a wallet. It was titled "The Librita." It appeared to be hand-bound in old, cracked, brown leather with leather straps.

"It is yours; no one else can touch it," said the spirit who had magically appeared beside him under the ceiling. DJ picked up the Librita and they both descended to the floor.

"You have the Book of Ancient Knowledge. You chose it and it chose you," said the spirit. "This book will keep you safe. Other spirits will attempt to get it from you, but beware not to give it to anybody. Always keep it close to you. Just remember, I will be here always. If you need me, the Librita will help you find me," he added. With that, the spirit vanished.

“Many other spirits inhabit the tower.”

— 3 —

The Enchanted Church Tower

DJ looked down at his new possession skeptically. Suddenly, a brilliant light emanated from the Librita and it seemed to float out of the palm of his hand. Then, incredibly, it began to expand. It opened in the middle and grew to the size of a small carpet. It floated about two feet off the ground right beside DJ and he felt compelled to sit on the enlarged book.

Immediately, DJ was transported by the magical book through the massive quarried stone wall of the Gothic church. It flew him outside and circled around the church a few times in an upward spiral. The dense fog had lifted and seemed to hover uncannily around the full moon. The spotlight on the ground lit up the church and its twin towers. The magic book banked like a plane and soared sideways into a narrow vent near the top of the right tower but DJ felt secure and did not feel as though he would fall off.

Inside, it was dark and DJ could smell the foul odor of bat dung. The bats were gone—hunting for the night. The light of the moon and the light of the spotlight on the church filtered through the vents so that he could see that thick cobwebs and black dust coated the entire interior of the church tower.

"When was the last time anyone came up here?" DJ's voice quivered and his heart pounded with anticipation. It was a rhetorical question. He was talking to himself and certainly did not expect an answer from the Book.

"Some time ago, in 1926, after the construction of this tower was completed," answered a deep melodic voice coming from the Book.

Shocked at the sound of another voice when he thought he was alone, DJ practically flew off the Book onto the floor.

"Whoa … you can talk!" DJ was stunned.

"Yes," answered the Book, "but you are the only one who can hear me." The Book continued, "Now that we have been introduced, what is it you want to know?"

DJ's thirst for answers was overpowering. "Okay. Why did you bring me up here? Can you explain to me what's going on with me, like seeing images, dreams and right here, talking to you?" he asked.

The Book replied, "The answer to your first question is that I wanted to bring you to a safe place away from prying evil eyes. Only good spirits live up here in the church tower. The answer to your second question is a bit more complicated."

"That's okay," said DJ. "I have time."

"You possess a power, but we have to determine where it originates," explained the Book.

"What do you mean by that?" asked DJ.

"Power comes from so many sources. We have to find out whether or not you are a wizard," answered the voice.

"How will I find that out?" DJ asked.

The Book did not answer. It just opened to its first page. The Book seemed to be alive. Surprisingly, its pages were not made of paper but consisted of a blend of materials like canvas, papyrus, bamboo film, and some interesting leaves. DJ did not know it then, but the characters in the book were a mixture of various ancient hieroglyphics: Celtic, Egyptian, Mayan, Incan, and Greek. It was impossible to read.

The Book of Ancient Knowledge instructed DJ to close his eyes, place his hand on the page, and read.

"How can I read if I close my eyes?" he queried.

The Book replied, "Will you trust me if I say you can?"

DJ followed the Book's instructions. He closed his eyes, placed his hand on the page and began to read aloud, "Book of Ancient Knowledge." When he opened his eyes again, the book was in the same form as it had been in the beginning … unreadable.

"Because you were able to read the words, I have determined that you are my master. Your handprint is now a part of me and I will open to you alone. You are truly a wizard and I am your aid. Keep me with you at all times and I will protect you and help you find the answers you seek," said the Book.

"If I am a wizard, where is my wand?" DJ had read about wizardry, had seen fictional wizard movies, and could only relate to what he had imagined. The Book understood this and decided that it was easiest for now to appease him.

"Oh, yes," it said. The Book then proceeded to shine a beam of light from its spine into a far dark corner of the tower room. There in the corner, along with some scattered dried leaves, lay a twig that looked as though it had landed there during a storm after blowing in through one of the church tower vents.

DJ went to retrieve it. The floor creaked. The tower room now brightly illuminated, DJ observed that it was empty except for a stone container covered in years of dust that was sitting prominently on a pedestal between two engraved pillars.

"What is that?" he asked.

"It is a vessel that contains the ashes of the key individual who built this church. His ghost resides in this tower," answered the Book. A shiver ran down DJ's spine and he could feel the hair on his arms stand at attention.

"Many other spirits inhabit the tower," continued the Book as if it was a common occurrence. "On All Souls Day, which is the first day of November, you can see them up here at midnight. There's a bossy one, a melancholy one, a workaholic, a craftsman, and an organizer, whom you have already met." DJ realized that in a couple of hours it would be the first day of November.

The Book continued. "There was a young priest whose life was cut short. He traveled, tirelessly helping the poor and the needy by bringing them food, clothing, and medicine. During one of his trips, he became ill and he walked thirty miles to get back here to Guelph. Then he died. He was a great missionary."

"That's sad," said DJ.

"Another soul that you should know about is that of the wood carver," continued the Book. "He was the man that lovingly carved all the statues and engravings inside and outside the church, including the carvings on the pillars you are looking at. He died in 1883 when he fell while working on the last carving on that tower. He was a great master craftsman."

The Book added, "This church is part of your own history. In 1888, the Church of Our Lady was changed and dedicated to Our Lady Immaculate. It is the place where your parents were married and you and your sister were baptized."

As soon as DJ picked up the oak twig, it straightened out and became a smooth piece of wood. It looked like one would expect a magic wand to look with a black handle and glowing emerald green tip. DJ was satisfied.

Standing near an open vent, DJ suddenly became aware of a commotion outside in the street below. He looked down through one of the slots in the vent and saw a gang of pirates harassing a glowing white skeleton.

"Hey, maties," said a gruff raspy voice, "we can use this guy for a flag on our mast!" A gang of about ten or twelve of his reveling "shipmates" joined in, surrounding the defenseless skeleton and the fun soon turned ugly.

DJ remembered that Nick had told him he was going to wear a cool skeleton costume that glowed in the dark.

"It's Nick!" he shouted. "He's in trouble! Please, get me down there, quick!"

DJ jumped on the Book and they magically flew through the thick tower wall and spiraled downward to the parking lot. Incredibly, no one had seen them descend. DJ jumped off the Book of Ancient Knowledge and it immediately shrunk down to its original wallet size and popped into DJ's pocket.

— 4 —

Magic Spells and Tragic Smells

DJ was one of the tallest kids in his class. Some kids called him D'Giant, instead of DJ. He was a little bit awkward because of his height. Girls were not interested in him, but some admired him for being good in sports, such as basketball, where his teammates affectionately referred to him as "Slam Dunkin' MacDonald." His real name was actually Duncan James MacDonald. On the volleyball team, his nickname was simply "Slam." He loved physical sports, especially hockey. He was big and strong for his age; that's why when he approached his friend, Nick seemed relieved to recognize DJ under all that pancake makeup.

Nick explained the situation. "I came looking for you, DJ, and this guy tripped me. He said I bumped into him on purpose so I apologized, but he and his buddies wouldn't let me pass."

"That's all you can say? 'Sorry.' Huh, loser?" Captain Eyepatch tried to incite a fight. His mangy crew played along and backed his story.

DJ said, "Look guys, it was an accident. You heard him—he's sorry." DJ tried to defuse the situation. Nevertheless, Captain Eyepatch was determined to start a fight and he would not ease up.

The pirate crew closed in on them. DJ and Nick had never seen them before. Since they were on so many sports teams together, they knew most kids their age in town, but these guys were not from here.

"This is not your fight, so shut up. You think because you're tall, you can scare me … us?" Captain Eyepatch said, gesturing to the other boys backing him.

"Look, we really don't want trouble here. Why don't we forget about what happened," said DJ, trying again to calm the situation. Nick was sweating. He found it difficult to handle bullying.

"Did you hear that, guys? This giant and his shadow are scared. Boohoo," he taunted. DJ looked at Nick and signaled him to calm down.

The instigated gang swarmed them. They pulled off DJ's cloak and one of them grabbed his iPod. DJ tried to grab it back but five of the gang members tackled him and then pinned him down.

He saw that Nick was struggling as they pinned him down on the ground, too. He suddenly remembered the magic wand. Where was it? Then he saw that one of the pirates was tossing it up in the air. DJ was furious, but he could not get free.

Then he noticed a van across the street. He closed his eyes to concentrate and mumbled something. All of a sudden, the van steered toward them. Its brakes did not work and it was speeding uncontrollably toward the crowd with the horn honking.

"Get out of the way!" shouted the driver. The crowd scattered in all directions. Then there was a big crash. DJ looked for Nick, but he could not find him. The van had run over the bully. He was screaming. His left leg was crushed. Others were slightly injured. Then DJ spotted Nick lying a few inches away from the van where it had come to a stop when it hit a tree. Steam was rising from under the hood of the van. DJ ran to Nick.

"Nick, are you okay? Please don't move," he said. His mom had made sure that he had learned first aid at an early age. Nick was trying to stand up.

"I'm okay … just a few scratches maybe," he said.

DJ went to see if he could help the bully who was still screaming. Blood was pouring out of his leg wound. DJ felt guilty. He had wished for the van to break up the crowd, but he did not expect it to hurt anyone. He applied pressure directly to the wound in an attempt to stop the bleeding, just as he had learned.

The ambulance came, siren blaring, emergency lights flashing. The paramedics thanked DJ for his quick thinking. They told him that he may have saved the boy's life and sped away to the hospital with Eyepatch.

"How ironic," thought DJ, but he did not say anything.

The police arrived—more sirens, more emergency lights. The crowd grew. The whole scene was chaotic. The police conducted an investigation, questioning witnesses, taking measurements, writing notes. Nobody wanted to say anything about the fight and nobody knew why the van had swerved into the crowd.

The driver was okay, but he was very shaken up. He explained to police that he seemed to have no control over the vehicle.

"Have you been drinking alcohol, sir?" the police officer asked the driver.

"No, officer. Something happened to the steering wheel and the brakes would not work," he explained. The police took more information. A tow truck was called to the scene.

The crowd soon dispersed. After they were interviewed by a police officer, DJ and Nick got permission from the officer to leave. As they walked back to campus, Nick explained to DJ that his dad's SUV got a flat tire on the way to the school earlier that evening and the battery in his cell phone had died so he was unable to call DJ to let him know he would be late. When he finally arrived at school, he looked for DJ. A vampire told him that he had seen DJ heading toward the mall.

"That's weird. I came looking for you when a vampire told me you were headed for the mall," said DJ.

Nick and DJ decided not to tell their parents what had happened for fear that they would not allow them to attend another school party. Nick went to the cafeteria to get a drink. DJ went to the washroom to wash the blood off his hands and to have a quiet moment to cool down, think, and avoid any further questions. He grabbed the Book from his pocket and was suddenly aware that he did not have the magic wand.

"Never mind," said the Book. "The wand is not magic. Your spell came from deep within you. It came from the magic of your will power—not from a stick."

DJ put the Book back into his pocket. He was very upset and muttered to himself, "What have I done? Nick was almost killed!" He wondered if he could have prevented the occurrence or if he could have reversed something bad. "Damn!" he hated what had happened. Maybe he was not ready for this magic business.

It was nearly midnight. The school party was breaking up and parents were picking up kids. DJ called his dad, who came to pick them up. Nick's dad had arranged with Alex to drive Nick home, as well.

"Have a good time?" asked Alex.

"Yeah, sure did," said the boys as they looked at each other. Then they were quiet while Hanna shared all her adventures of the evening.

After dropping Nick off, they drove home. As they turned into their own driveway, DJ spotted a skunk in the headlights near the garage. Without much effort, he turned the skunk into a cat. Neither Alex nor Hanna had noticed the skunk.

Laura was still up waiting to hear how the party went. Hanna was delighted to relate the night's events again.

Alex came in mumbling something about a cat sitting in front of the garage door that stank like hell. Hanna ran outside to see the cat. Approaching it, she covered her nose.

"What are you doing here, cat? Are you hungry?" She went back inside and returned with food and water.

Laura and Alex went out to check the smelly cat. "Is it a he or a she?" asked Laura.

"Not sure," answered Alex.

DJ came out to look at the cat. His suspicions were correct. It was indeed the skunk cat. He pretended he had never seen it before.

"Don't worry, it will disappear tomorrow," he said, but he was wrong. The friendly cat stayed in the garage and Alex named it Smelly Cat. Kibbles and Smelly Cat became buddies. Smelly liked to eat Kibbles' food, and Kibbles did not mind sharing.

— 5 —

Hockey Horror

It was the dead of winter. The MacDonalds were counting down the days to their South Seas vacation. Southern Ontario was blanketed with nearly a foot of fresh snow. The Guelph Ice Storm hockey team had a tough new coach, Mr. Bill Saunders. He spit and cursed a lot, but he had brought the team out of the cellar by putting DJ and Nick together on the first line. Now the team had come up through the ranks to second in the league.

DJ and Nick had met one Saturday morning many years ago when they were trying out for Tykes Minor League at the skating arena. They clicked and became friends forever. Nick's mom and dad, Andrea and Gerry, became good friends with Laura and Alex. Today, the proud dads sat with excited anticipation behind the Ice Storm's bench.

It was 7:30 PM on Wednesday evening. The weather was calm and cold but pleasant. They had a big game against the Supreme Cyclones at their competitor's arena. This team had a reputation for being very rough and bullish. They were crass and arrogant but ranked as the best team in the league. Their two defense boys were the scariest kids you have ever seen. They should have played football instead of hockey. They were each a husky six feet tall at the age of thirteen or fourteen.

After the national anthem, the whistle blew and the puck was dropped. The atmosphere was very intense. The arena was full and the spectators cheered their teams. Fans were excited. They were jeering, booing, screaming, and whistling. This was not to be a typical hockey game.

From the start, the parents of the Supreme Cyclones team started yelling, "Get him! Get him!" Nick was the left forward. He got the pass from DJ, and then he was checked into the boards. They were trying to break him down. Alex and Gerry watched their boys and started to get concerned. The game resumed and the same thing happened—one body check after another. It was clear that the opposing team had a plan to break them all night.

At the end of the first period neither team had scored. The Ice Storm coach, Mr. Saunders, briefed the team during intermission. He was angry that the other team was playing so dirty and told his team to change their strategy. He yelled at them red-faced, arms flailing, and demanded a goal. Big pressure was put on DJ.

The whistle blew and the players went back on the ice again. DJ was determined to score for the team. The puck dropped and went to the opponents who attempted a pass, but the Ice Storm's right forward, number twenty-one, intercepted it. He sped to the Supreme Cyclones' net, where he was poked in the ribs and hooked on his right leg by a defenseman. He flew like a derailed train, hit the boards, and fell face down. His mother and father were screaming in disbelief. The referee called the team trainer to administer first aid. The boy was groaning. He was bleeding from above his left eyebrow. They helped him off the ice. He would be all right, but he would not play again in that game. The Ice Storm needed a replacement, while the Supreme Cyclones got off with a two-minute penalty for hooking.

When play resumed, DJ was full of adrenaline. With an end-to-end rush, he scored. The second period ended 1–0.

During the third period of play, there was intense passing and checking. The Supreme Cyclones got a goal, bringing the score to 1–1. A penalty was called against the Ice Storm. The Supreme Cyclones scored again. The Ice Storm needed another replacement, this time a defenseman. The team rallied. They concentrated on good skating, checking, and passing. DJ moved quickly and scored to tie the Supreme Cyclones. The leader board showed the new score of 2–2. They needed one more goal to break the tie. With ten minutes remaining in the game, the Ice Storm scored. The crowd was going crazy.

With three minutes remaining, the Supreme Cyclones got control of the puck. They passed it to center, to left, and back to center. On the pass to right, Nick stole the puck and caught the other team off guard. Nick and DJ stormed down the ice on a breakaway. Nick passed the puck to DJ. Then out of the corner of his eye, DJ saw something terrible happen.

The huge Supreme Cyclone defenseman gave Nick a heavy body check and he went flying. The other defenseman was swooping down on DJ. The crowd roared, "Get him! Get him!" With a loud crash, DJ was thrown to the ice. He was shaken and hurting, but he tried to stand up. He was dazed. Then images from his dreams began to merge with reality. He saw an ugly and scary creature beating on Nick. In a flash, he stood up with a growl. He could sense that blood was rushing to his eyes but all he could think of was saving his best friend. He flew over, pounced on this "creature," and punched him repeatedly as hard as he could. Then, summoning all his strength, DJ lifted him up and threw him into the corner. Without realizing it, DJ had beaten up the big Supreme Cyclones boy.

The roaring crowd seemed like a distant blur. Players from both teams pulled off their gloves and began to fight. Some of the spectators jumped onto the ice, pushing, shoving, and yelling at each other. Those left in the stands began to throw things onto the rink. In all the chaos, Alex and Gerry made their way to the ice to defend their sons. The referee had rushed to the initial fight between DJ and the Supreme Cyclones player, but had arrived too late to stop the beating. He and the linemen tried to calm the crowd, stop all the fights, and defuse the tension. Finally, they regained control of the situation. An ambulance was called and DJ stood there frozen. This time he had really lost it. He knew it. He sat on the bench. He was exhausted and confused. He cradled his head in his bloody hands and sobbed.

It was a total nightmare. The ambulance came and went. The police came and took DJ to the station. Alex went with him. Gerry took Nick to the hospital to be checked over. He called his wife and Laura to meet them at the hospital. Nick was very quiet. He was upset over what had happened. It was not DJ's fault, but he wondered why DJ had to beat that kid so hard and how he had summoned all that strength and power. He had overheard some of the other guys on their team talking. They were upset that the team might be disqualified from the rest of the tournament.

In the morning, the incident was all over the front page of the *Guelph Mercury* newspaper. The rest of the province's news network picked up the story as well. The MacDonalds' home phone had not stopped ringing since the early morning. There were calls of concern from the school principal, some teachers, and family friends. There were calls from classmates who supported DJ's fight. There were calls from complete strangers who called him names and said nasty things about him. DJ went to his room and locked the door.

When Alex became aware that the paparazzi were in their front yard trying to get a picture of any member of the family, he called police to secure their privacy. Laura drank her tea while pacing back and forth in the kitchen. Alex stood and watched outside. His right arm was leaning on the island in the kitchen. Laura's eyes were moist. She asked Alex if they should call a lawyer for legal advice.

A few days passed. On Saturday afternoon at half past four, DJ put on his jacket and went down to the lake with his hockey stick, a pair of skates and a puck in hand. It would be dark by 5:00 PM, but he needed some fresh air. He made sure that no one was outside to watch him, especially the paparazzi. The lake had frozen over. He skated back and forth on the ice. His heart was aching with anger and frustration. Why was he having such bad dreams that seemed so real? Was it because no one in his family believed him? In whom could he confide? Whom could he trust? He skated around the frozen lake, thinking. He had the urge to scream, hoping that the ugly creature from the arena would reappear. Where had it come from?

"Yes, why didn't I think of that!" He checked his pocket, but the Librita was not there. "I have to find it," he said to himself as he rushed back to the house.

Laura had taken a few days off work to try to figure out this mess. She decided to speak with her mother in the Philippines just for the comfort of hearing her voice. As a matter of pride, she had never discussed family issues with anyone, not even her mother, but this time she really needed to confide in someone. She explained to her mother about all the terrible visions DJ had been having and the horrible things that had been happening. Her mom tried to comfort her as best she could over the phone and reassured her that everything would turn out all right. It was around 5:00 PM She confirmed the time that they were arriving in the Philippines for the reunion.

Alex finally talked to a number of lawyers and decided on one he thought could best represent DJ. Her name was Connie Law. She had a reputation for being the best defense lawyer and she was respected in their community. She had represented various NHL players in cases similar to DJ's.

As a result of apologies, appealing to the mercy of the court, and negotiations with the court, DJ was allowed to go on vacation with his parents. The one-month trip would be a part of his rehabilitation period. He also promised to do public service work at the drop-in center on Gordon Street, every Saturday when he came back from the Philippine trip.

— 6 —

Secrets Shared in Shangri-la

The trip to the Philippines was a break for all of them, especially DJ. Perhaps all these terrible things were just happening here in Canada. Perhaps his luck would change if he went far away. Kibbles and Smelly Cat were being taken care of by Nick and his family. It seemed like a vacation to them, as well.

After nineteen hours and twenty-five minutes of flying, the pilot made an announcement on the speaker requesting that the passengers get back to their seats in preparation for landing. Five minutes later, the landing gear was released. DJ could see a few islands from his window. They were flying over Lantau Island. He could see the runway. It appeared to be floating on the water. The plane landed perfectly. The passengers applauded the captain as his voice came on the speaker welcoming everyone to Hong Kong.

The high-tech airport was big but organized. It did not take them too long to reach the gate for Philippine Airlines. The connecting flight would take them from Hong Kong to Cebu in the Philippines. Counter crews were very helpful and polite. The family decided to look in the duty-free shops. Laura said that they needed a little exercise for proper blood circulation. Half an hour later, in addition to blood circulation, a monetary circulation had occurred. Soon after, they were aboard the plane to Cebu.

It was a pleasant flight. Both DJ and Hanna were very attentive to what was below. Although they occasionally fought like cat and mouse, when things got rough, they stuck together and supported each other. Back home, things had not been easy for Hanna either. She had become known as "the sister of the boy who was arrested for beating a guy to a pulp." This change of scenery seemed to be just what they needed. Hanna had a window seat and got so excited taking pictures with her digital camera that she filled half her memory card.

Some distant relatives of the family met them at Mactan Airport in Cebu on Lapu-lapu Island and told them that Laura's sister, Evelyn, her husband, Liam, and their children, Joshua and Emma, the O'Leary family from the United States, had arrived two days earlier and had already moved on to El Nido. After such long hours in flight, the MacDonalds needed to relax and unwind. A van whisked them to Shangri-la Hotel. It was only about fifteen minutes from the airport. They drove on narrow Punta Engano Road past houses and small convenience stores. Multi-cab vans and other passenger vans congested the road. The driver of their van gave them a brief history of Mactan. He pointed out a monument of Lapu-lapu, the one-time chieftain of the island of Mactan. This was where Magellan, the Spanish explorer, had discovered the Philippines in 1521. Lapu-lapu had killed Magellan on this shore but not before Magellan had schemed with the other tribes to murder Lapu-lapu. According to history, Lapu-lapu was decapitated and his head was displayed for days at this gate of the shore.

While listening to this short history lesson, DJ and Hanna embraced the smells in the air, which were a blend of the earth and the seawater. The sights overwhelmed them. It had been a long time since they had last visited the country. On that visit, they had landed in Manila. DJ was about seven years old when he first came to visit his Grandpa and Lola (the Filipino name for Grandma) in the Philippines.

It was overcast and a humid thirty degrees. It was the perfect time to go for a swim. According to ads, the Shangri-la was "set amid fourteen hectares of lush tropical greenery." The hotel staff was very friendly. When they entered the lobby, DJ and his dad felt out of place. They were more than a foot taller than most of the Filipino men they encountered. They felt like towering giants. Of course, Laura blended right in. You could see on her face that she felt at home again.

After checking in, a bellman helped them carry their luggage to their room. DJ and Hanna shared a room with two queen-sized beds and had an access door to their parents' room. Their mom and dad instructed them to get the things they would need for three days. Laura's relatives were waiting to take their suitcases directly to El Nido Island in order to make their traveling more comfortable during the following days. With no choice, there they were, unpacking and repacking. A frustrated Hanna could not make up her mind about what to keep. DJ had packed his secret magic book, the Librita, and made sure to keep it with him. The rest of the family still had no knowledge of its existence.

It was around 10:00 AM when they finally settled down. Alex suggested that they go down to the swimming pool to have a quick swim, a light lunch, and a nap. He reminded them that they were adjusting to a twelve-hour time difference from back home, which meant that it was exactly 10:00 PM in Guelph.

The hotel was packed with tourists from Japan, Hong Kong, China, and Korea. There were some Europeans and an Arab with a briefcase who appeared to be a businessman. DJ and Hanna were walking toward the pool when some Japanese men dressed in diving gear passed by on their way back from the beach. Curious as to what it looked like out there, DJ and Hanna went to the white sand beach of Cebu while their parents stayed at the pool.

The ocean was calm. They could see their own reflections in the clear water. DJ tapped the water with his toes. It was perfect. He looked into the distance and unexpectedly, he saw the reflection of the sun smiling and saying, "Welcome." He stepped back. Hanna asked DJ if he was all right. He nodded but retreated and ran back to the pool. Hanna called to him. When he did not answer, she mumbled to herself and ran after him.

Their parents were already in the pool chatting with other people. Alex introduced DJ and Hanna and they responded with a quiet hello.

"What's the matter, sweetie?" Laura asked Hanna.

She could tell from Hanna's face that she was upset with her brother, but DJ looked straight at her and she replied, "Nothing." She looked at her brother with a "you're going to pay for this later" kind of stare.

After a short twenty-minute swim, they went back to their rooms to change for lunch. DJ put on his white Guess shirt, khaki shorts, and flip-flops. He was checking his hair in a hallway mirror, while Hanna was changing in the bathroom. Hanna demanded an explanation. Even though her voice was muffled coming from the bathroom, DJ shut the access door to their parents' room hoping they had not overheard her.

He stood in front of the bathroom door, turned around, leaned his back against it, and said, "Okay, I will explain everything later. Now, are you satisfied? Such a monkey!" he muttered.

They took the elevator down, passed through the lobby and went down a stairway to the restaurant for a buffet lunch. Laura reminded her family to take it easy since their systems were still confused about the timing. It was 12:15 PM, but as far as their bodies were concerned, they should be sleeping—not having lunch. They all agreed that the meal was excellent.

Before heading back upstairs to nap, Laura suggested that they take a few minutes to walk around the garden. She was admiring the beautiful hibiscus, bougainvilleas, anthurium, bird of paradise blooms, and ivy plants that draped from the pergola posts. DJ and Hanna excused themselves and went to their room. Alex and Laura sat on a bench, listening to the trickling fountain in front of them. Laura leaned on Alex's shoulder and said, "I hope this vacation will do him good."

"He seems okay, doesn't he?" Alex asked. She nodded and he gave her a light kiss on the lips.

Hanna had the key to the room and she led her brother inside. She pleaded with him to tell her what was going on. He hesitated but then he looked her in the eyes and said, "Only if you promise me that this will be our secret."

She offered her baby finger to him and pledged, "I promise." Then she positioned herself on the bed as if she were going to hear a bedtime story. DJ pushed the access door keeping it slightly ajar so that they would know when their parents came in.

DJ told Hanna about the intense dreams that he had been having for the past year and described them to her in detail. He was seeing old places, beautiful and ugly faces, and the weirdest enormous and tiny creatures that one could imagine. At times, he could see another world. He seemed to be there in reality, floating under the sea and communicating with odd creatures and something seemed to be calling him. Something or someone needed his help.

"I don't have any freakin' clue why," he continued. "I can't help it. Images just pop up on the screen of my computer, in the street, and at hockey. It seems like the images are following me everywhere I go. Would you like to know what happened out there on the beach? I saw the sun's reflection in the water smiling and saying 'welcome' to me. I'm not some sort of crazy lunatic or druggie or whatever," he added. "These visions seem very real. I can almost touch them."

"I know," said Hanna. Then, to DJ's amazement, Hanna confided that she had been having a recurring dream about an undersea gathering of mermaids and in her dream, she was one of them. She said that although the dream was not frightening like DJ's, she had been dreaming the same vivid dream every night for the past week.

Then DJ showed her the Librita and explained how it had come into his possession and what had happened on Halloween. Hanna was stunned and looked at him in awe. DJ was sincerely and visibly upset and she had no problem believing him.

They heard footsteps and another door opened down the hall. Hanna pulled up the bed cover and DJ jumped on his bed and acted as if he were asleep. Hanna whispered in her tiny voice, "If you see things, wake me up." Then she closed her eyes. Laura came to check on them and set the alarm clock in their room to ring at 4:30 PM so that they would not miss the beach activities later in the afternoon.

They had a great time at the beach and an early night seemed to get their systems back on a normal schedule.

— 7 —

Legend of the Landlocked Lake

The next morning, Hanna asked her brother if he had had any more dreams during the night. He could hardly believe that for the past two or three nights, including his sleep aboard the plane, he had had no nightmares—only the daytime image of the sun welcoming him.

A relative had given Laura a local cell phone so that they could communicate with the rest of the family. Lola called to say hello to everyone. Laura was first to talk to her mother, then she passed the phone to Alex, Hanna, and DJ. DJ spoke to his grandma from the veranda of their room. Lola's voice comforted him. Although she had a thick accent and her English was limited, he understood almost everything she tried to convey to him. Both kids could hardly wait to see their Lola and Lolo. DJ preferred to call his Lolo "Grandpa."

After packing, checking, and making sure they were not leaving anything behind, they went downstairs to check out of the Shangri-la; however, Laura's relative had already checked them out and a van was waiting for them outside. They would have one more plane ride and then they would see the rest of the family.

Mactan International Airport was small but clean. It had been built by a Japanese company. Three of Laura's relatives joined them. Laura spoke to them in their dialect and inquired about their families. The flight was on time. Off they flew to El Nido.

Inside the plane, DJ chose a window seat. He wanted to see what the island looked like from the sky. The plane was old and small and he did not recognize the name of the manufacturer. The seats were cramped and the ceiling was low. As they flew in the noisy plane, DJ noticed that his dad was fidgeting. He had his gaze fixed on the cockpit, and looked at his watch often. He seemed worried. The air conditioner was rumbling and the air inside the plane was stale.

Everyone on the plane was sweating. DJ began to feel sick. He closed his eyes but that made him feel worse. Embarrassed to disturb his mom or anybody, he looked for a piece of gum inside his pocket. His hand touched the Librita instead. He held it tightly and wished for a comfortable plane ride. Suddenly, there was a big bang coming from the air conditioning unit, and, amazingly, it began to work. The cabin of the plane cooled off and everyone was able to breathe fresh air. DJ's feeling of nausea went away. The Librita was true to its word and had looked out for him again.

When the other passengers became excited and pointed out of their windows, DJ looked down through the window at the beautiful tropical islands below. He saw hundreds of odd-shaped brown hills that looked like Hershey chocolate cups floating in a turquoise power drink.

"What are those?" asked one passenger behind DJ who had never been there before either.

With a giddy voice, another replied, "Locals call them chocolate hills, but I prefer to call them lava cakes."

DJ looked at his map. A distant relative named Julio, who was sitting beside him, said, "We are above Bohol Island," and helped him locate it on the map.

The plane cruised to a low altitude, and the scenery below became clear and discernible. There were a couple of ferries moving on the calm sea. One was heading north and one south. A few fishing boats were idling near the shore. The blue-green color of the ocean was captivating and they could see for miles.

As they approached the tip of El Nido Island, DJ's heart began to race, but he did not know why. He looked down again. One particular island caught his attention. It was a coral rock mountain partially covered with brush and trees with a lake right in the middle. The pointy column dominated the skyline, as this was the tallest of all the islands. Julio began to relate the local legend of the interior lake to him.

"The locals swear that the lake is enchanted and that the sparkling water is really the sun glistening on treasure that lies just below the surface of the water," he said. "The legend maintains that there are about a dozen tunnels that lead through the mountain to this landlocked lake. Each has dangerous obstacles like fire-breathing snakes, bottomless pits, and natural booby traps, to deter looters and prevent them from reaching the lake. There is only one secret tunnel leading directly to the enchanted lake without any obstacles or dangers. Finding this secret tunnel, however, is nearly impossible. To this day, no one has been successful in reaching the lake and finding the gold and jewels that are rumored to be hidden there. Any adventurer that has attempted to reach the lake via a tunnel, has never been seen since then. It is feared that all who have entered the tunnels have succumbed to the deadly obstacles that lurk within the mountain."

DJ was fascinated by the legend. Julio sounded like an expert on the area. A passenger sitting across the aisle, who had overheard Julio's tale, began to ask him questions. Their voices faded as DJ looked down again to the island with the sparkling lake in the middle.

It was déjà vu. DJ felt as though he had been there before. He was immediately consumed by another vivid vision: It was the middle of the day. A waterproof camera hung on his neck as he was surfing on the ocean. The waves brought him to that island. There was a narrow strip of white, sandy beach on one side, perhaps due to the low tide. He wandered around, taking pictures and admiring the privacy and serenity. He touched the base of the coral mountain. It was prickly—not a good idea to climb. He noticed a bird's nest on a branch of a tree and took a photograph. Strange sounds were coming from within the nest so he wanted to see what was inside. Underneath the branch was a four-foot wide crack in the coral. To satisfy his curiosity, DJ tried to balance himself on his tiptoes on the brushes that grew on one side of the cavity. Suddenly, a huge green frog leaped from underneath the brush. It startled him off balance and he fell through the crack into the water.

The water was cold and before he could grasp the sides of the cavity, the strong current pulled him away. The water was getting colder and colder as the current carried him through a labyrinth of coral and into a tunnel. The tunnel narrowed until it was only two yards wide. Because of the narrowing artery, the current rushed faster. Suddenly, as the passage dipped below water level, the entire tunnel was flooded. DJ held his breath. He knew that he could not fight the undercurrent, so he let it carry him and hoped that his lungs would not run out of air before he reached a higher level in the tunnel. After more than two minutes under water, his lungs felt as though they would burst. Then suddenly, the current seemed to spit him up out of the water. He found himself floating in the middle of the lake. He could feel his body getting stronger and stronger. The lake sparkled like diamonds. It was very bright.

DJ's vision was abruptly interrupted when the flight attendant asked him to fasten his seatbelt in preparation for landing.

El Nido's airport was tiny and not as advanced as the high-tech airports of the western hemisphere. Even though the plane's air conditioner was now working, Alex was still sweating. As he looked down at the tiny runway from a distance, he wondered how they could land on that "postage stamp." The runway was shorter but the pilot managed to land the plane without a hiccup. About twenty passengers disembarked from the plane.

Lola and three of her grandchildren came to meet them at the airport. With tears of joy, she gave them warm hugs and expressed her happiness to see her daughter and her family again. DJ's uncle had arranged for a couple of SUVs for the next part of the trip. The adults got into one of the vehicles while DJ, Hanna, and their three cousins, Aboud, Farrah, and Venus, got into the other. Aboud and Farrah were the children of Laura's sister Maya and Amir Al Shammari. They had come from Jordan for the reunion. Venus was the daughter of Laura's sister Marissa and her husband, Adonis, who were here from Greece.

The drivers drove them down a narrow and winding road. The asphalt seemed new. There were only a few houses on either side. When the car stopped at the end of the road, they all got into a yellow Sea Ray tied to the dock. The cousins were excited to see each other again and were amazed at how much they had changed over the past four years. They were planning with whom and in which rooms they would be bunking. Passersby took a glimpse at the westerners and laughed.

The boat was loaded. Another small boat was loaded with water in plastic bottles and other supplies: pop, San Miguel Beer, live chickens, and fresh vegetables. The Sea Ray was big enough to hold at least ten people and it was not a long boat ride.

In the distance, they could see many islands of different shapes. The island beaches consisted of pure white sand that stretched for miles and miles along the shorelines. It was paradise. This untouched virgin beauty of the islands was the Philippines' best-kept secret.

— 8 —

Disappearance in Malipayon Cove

They finally reached Grandpa's island: Malipayon Cove. The island was about fifteen hectares in area. The towering mountain rocks protected the buildings from the midday sun and sometimes the cold, strong wind from the north. The rocky mountain cliffs fringed by a thick tropical primary forest, were home to unusual flora and fauna. One could catch an early morning glimpse of a variety of birds and animals.

It looked like a scene on a postcard. There was a big dock and boardwalk. The main building was on a hill that overlooked the beachfront. It was constructed with traditional materials of hardwood, bamboo, and thatched roof, which were all locally sourced. This was where the family gathered for dining, socializing, and card games. About twenty small cottages surrounded the main building. They were nestled in shady alcoves among palm trees and other tropical vegetation. In the midst of these buildings sat a gigantic swimming pool. There was a separate building called a media room that housed half a dozen computer arcade games for back-up entertainment when the weather was bad. Across from the media room, there was another building, the shop. Uncle Godfrey, Laura's youngest brother who still lived on the island with his wife, Lee Yan, had collections of interesting shells, unusual rocks, and shapes of wood. In his leisure time, he loved to create things, like ornaments in the shop. There was a gym with a fitness room, a pool hall, and a half-court for basketball.

Almost everyone had arrived except Laura's sister, Mariana, who was flying in from Vancouver with her husband, Ishwar, and their daughter, Noor. Laura's brother, Peter, and his wife, Yvonne, had yet to arrive with their daughters, Nadia and Jelina, from Switzerland. Apparently, there were delays in their flights from Vancouver and Switzerland. Each family was designated a cottage of its own, but the cousins negotiated with Lola to have one for the teenage girls and one for the teenage boys. The trick in this family was that Lola always had the last word and Lolo always supported what she said. When Lola said yes, it was a definite yes. The girls were looking forward to catching up on their girly talks without adults being around. The boys were also looking forward to their privacy without adults interfering.

The kids moved their suitcases to their own cottages. All eleven of Laura's siblings were coming to this family reunion. None of them had ever missed even one. They had a close relationship with each other. Looking at her own children brought back memories of when she was growing up. Laura convinced herself that DJ was fine after all.

Alex disappeared into the kitchen to "inspect the facilities," he said. When he reappeared from the kitchen, he had a platter in his hands and grinned at his wife. The cook had prepared some fish—just caught an hour earlier. He had helped himself to a beer and called to the rest of the guys standing by the bay.

Laura, her siblings, and their spouses gathered at the cabana. Lee Yan, Godfrey's wife, requested a house punch served with some finger foods from the staff. They talked about how beautiful the place looked and expressed their gratitude for Lola and Lolo's hospitality in planning this event. The siblings teased and play-wrestled then had a few more drinks. The ladies enjoyed drinking fresh coconut water right from the husk.

It was Easter season. Today was Holy Thursday. As far back as anyone could remember, Lola and Lolo practiced the tradition of abstaining from eating red meat until Saturday. Most meals consisted of different kinds of fish and shellfish.

It was almost three o'clock in the afternoon when they got a call from Peter and Mariana Their families had met in Manila and were traveling together to El Nido. It would take about an hour flight to get there and there would be plenty of time for cocktails. Grandpa asked the men to fetch them at the airport. Lola went to the kitchen to instruct the staff what to cook for dinner. That evening's menu included lobster, crab, and shrimp.

The older kids hit the beach and the little ones were at the swimming pool.

The tables were set for twenty-six adult family members, twenty kids, and a couple dozen staff. Everyone found a seat. Little kids had their own table. The adults mixed with the household help and sat with them at every table. It was a house rule that everybody should be seated at the table, including the help. "The family that eats together, stays together" was their motto. Then one of the little granddaughters volunteered to say grace.

Dinner consisted of steamed lobster, crab with red chili and ginger, sautéed shrimp mixed with veggies, fish soup, and rice. Dessert was a mixture of tropical fruits: lanzones, mangousteen, rambuttan, pineapple, and watermelon. It was a delicious meal. Before they left the table, one of the grandsons said a "Thank You" prayer.

After dinner, Grandpa called for a general gathering in the family room. The walls were decorated with framed country flags: Canada, the United States, Scotland, Germany, China, Ireland, Mexico, Spain, Italy, Kenya, India, Switzerland, Japan, Jordan, Greece, England, France, and the Philippines. Entering that room felt like going to a United Nations convention. Lola was very proud of her grandchildren's heritage and her blended family.

Grandpa gave a brief welcome speech. It was followed by a short speech by Laura because she was the oldest child in the family, then Alex, and then the rest of the siblings. The speeches were followed by gift giving. It was an Easter tradition to exchange gifts between cousins, uncles, aunts, and the other members of the household. This was a fun time. It felt like Christmas. DJ got a guitar from Uncle

Godfrey as an advanced birthday gift, and Hanna got quite a few gifts from cousins and aunts.

Afterward, Lola amused herself by playing solitaire. The men went to the game room and played a round of billiards while talking business and politics. The ladies lounged in the family room, catching up about kids, work, and travel. Laura asked for suggestions for DJ's birthday the next day. She thought they could plan some parlor games to make it interesting, which was what they used to do as children.

The younger kids went to bed. The six teenage girls went to their cottage, decided on their bunking arrangements, and talked about boys, bands, and boy bands. The younger ones, Hanna, Kirsten, Nadia, and Emma, all aged thirteen or fourteen, listened to funny dating stories told by Venus, age seventeen and Farrah, age nineteen.

The teen boys hung out at the beach and played the new guitar. DJ strummed the instrument and Hans played the melody while Aboud, Joshua, Takanori, and Sammi were goofing around to the music. It was a real comedy act. There were conversations about school, sports, and girls. The bonfire was still burning around 10:00 PM when they saw some members of the household staff preparing the small motor boats to go out. The boys asked them where they were going.

"Fishing," one responded. "There's a full moon and it is the right time to catch squid." The boys got excited and wanted to go out with them.

One ran up the path and asked permission from the adults and Grandpa said, "Okay, but don't be long. Be back before midnight." The staff prepared three motor boats, kerosene lamps, and life jackets.

The water was calm. The temperature had dropped to comfortable in the gentle ocean breeze. Out here, away from city lights, they saw billions of stars and experienced the awesome feeling of being a part of the universe. Only the quiet humming of the electric trolling motors and the wavelets that lapped the sides of the boats broke the silence. In the distance, tiny red lights sparkled in the ocean. One of the boys asked what that was, and a voice replied in almost a reverent whisper, "Fishermen."

Their fishing lines trolled behind the boats as they neared the other fishermen. It was a humbling experience for the boys to witness how these local people caught whatever fish they could to trade at the market in the morning. They dropped their nets and in no time, they were full of fish. Most of them were squid. The creatures were all alive. They were jumping and trying to go back to the ocean. For all of the boys, this was their first experience fishing at night.

While the fishermen celebrated their catch, DJ suddenly had the peculiar sensation that the ocean was swallowing them all. His heart began to race. He looked at everyone, but their actions indicated that they were unaware of DJ's fears and they continued to enjoy the fishing.

Then Hans, who was sitting across from DJ, glanced over to him and noticed the strange look on his face. He sensed that DJ was uncomfortable. "Maybe it's the motion of the rocking boat," he thought.

Hans looked at his watch and suggested that they head back to the cottage as Grandpa had told them. They had caught a full bucket of squid and four red snappers. The boys were very proud of their catch. They all said good night to the other fishermen and headed back to the island. They had been gone almost two hours but it felt like only twenty minutes.

The men docked the boats and brought the night's spoils to the kitchen of the main house. Takanori and Sammi said they were wiped and went to the cottage to crash for the night. They had been up for almost twenty-three hours.

DJ, Hans, Aboud, and Joshua decided to stay at the dock a few more minutes to enjoy the full moon that was shining down on them. Its spectacular reflection danced on the waves and mesmerized them. Then Aboud, who was four years older than DJ, took the guitar out of its case and began to strum. He picked up the beat and the other three began to dance foolishly when Hans accidentally bumped DJ. DJ tried to balance himself on the edge of the dock and grabbed Hans to keep from falling into the water. It all seemed to happen in slow motion. The two of them made a big splash in the water that was about seven or eight feet deep by the dock. Fortunately, both boys were good swimmers. Aboud and Joshua roared with laughter as they watched DJ and Hans gulp the salty water.

Then something strange happened. When DJ fell, he stepped on something lying on the ocean floor. He reached down, grabbed it, and brought it back to the surface. Hans was already climbing back onto the dock. DJ showed the others what he had found. Both Joshua and Aboud examined the object out of curiosity but did not think too much of it. Hans, on the other hand, was fascinated. He examined it closely. It was a shell of an oyster in the shape of a crown. It was a very unusual looking piece and Joshua suggested that they show it to Uncle Godfrey. Knowing his artistic talent and artisanship, they thought that he might make something out of it.

Hans took the object from DJ. On a whim, he held it over DJ's head as if to crown him. He was just trying to be funny and to tease him but a bizarre thing happened: a bright dazzling light from the moon zapped DJ and Hans like a laser and they were gone.

— 9 —

The Mysterious Other World

The other two cousins, Aboud and Joshua, were petrified by what they had seen. Two men who had been sitting on the veranda of a cottage watching from a distance were alarmed and bolted from their seats. One of them, Julio, sprinted toward the main house. Inside, a few adults were still awake, drinking tea or adult drinks, and talking. Some of the others had already gone back to their cottages and were preparing to sleep.

Julio flung open the door without knocking. Grandpa and Lola stood up from their seats, "What's wrong?" Grandpa asked.

Gasping for breath, Julio replied, "Please come down to the dock. DJ and Hans are both gone."

Lola looked at the clock on the wall and it was two minutes past midnight. It was DJ's birthday and he was fifteen that day. She looked at Grandpa. Their eyes met and she said, "The time has come."

Upon hearing this, the parents of the two boys were stunned. Alex asked, "Did I hear right? Both boys are gone! Gone where?"

Fritz Schroeder, Hans' father, added, horrified, "Do you mean they drowned?" He threw his hands up in the air. Panic gripped the room.

"Listen everyone," said Lola, "Let's go down to the dock."

Alex and Fritz stormed out, followed by the others. Normally, it was about a three-minute walk down to the dock but they were running. Aboud and Joshua met them half way. They were still in shock. They told the adults what they had witnessed as they all rushed to the dock.

There was total chaos. Fritz was furious and wanted to report the incident to the police or perhaps the coast guard. Laura began to cry and mumbled that it was all her fault. Alex was almost hysterical. Then, Grandpa stopped everyone from talking with his commanding voice. He was always a very gentle and soft-spoken man. They rarely heard such an authoritative voice come from him.

"Listen to me now. Both boys are fine and I assure you on my own life, they will come back," he said with conviction. His children all began talking again at the same time. He cut them off, saying, "Yes, Fritz, you have a question."

Fritz replied, "How can you assure us that they are coming back?" His German tone demanded an answer. His wife, Carmelita, embraced him.

Grandpa ordered, "Everybody follow me." They followed him back up to the main house.

Meanwhile, DJ and Hans were floating in an air bubble at an extremely fast speed but they could not tell whether they were going up or down. Hans noticed that DJ's appearance had changed. He looked like royalty, a prince perhaps. His crown was made of soft coral wrapped with a turban-like material with various precious stones attached to it. He was clothed in a golden velvet robe. Hans also observed that DJ had a sword at his side, but DJ was unaware of it. With a bowing gesture, Hans was trying to tell him that he looked funny but DJ did not pay attention.

The air bubble began to slow down. It was dark. They tried to determine where they were but could not see anything. The two of them stood side-by-side and squinted to see outside the bubble but saw only darkness. Suddenly, DJ saw something move. In a double take, he looked again but whatever it was had disappeared. The bubble stopped for a few seconds.

"DJ, where are we?" Hans nudged DJ but he did not reply. He was concerned with what was happening outside of the bubble. A part of his brain told him that this was another dream. DJ suddenly gasped and grabbed Hans' arm and pointed out what was in front of them.

There, towering directly in front of the boys was an enormous, monstrous creature. DJ recognized it as one of the evil creatures he had seen in his dreams. He called it an ogre for lack of a better name. It had the head of a snake, the body of a human covered in scales, hands, the feet of a crocodile, and a long tongue. It had a ten-foot long tail that curled and a fin like a fish on its back. They were in stunned disbelief. Where were they?

"Is this for real?" DJ asked himself.

Hans said in a whisper, "Pinch me, DJ. If this is a dream I want to wake up." DJ looked at him and raised his hand to pinch Hans, but the bubble bounced in wave turbulence so Hans grabbed DJ's arm to balance their footing.

Then they realized that the creature was not alone but there appeared to be thousands of them. Luckily, the creatures seemed to be unaware of their presence. They looked as if they were asleep or in a state of suspended animation and could not see or hear them.

In a whisper, DJ said to Hans, "I've seen this creature before. Have you ever heard any strange voices or seen images like this in your dreams?" However, before Hans could reply, the bubble began to move in another direction and DJ saw another image from one of his dreams. It was a cage made of about forty solid rock pillars.

"DJ, I have been having nightmares lately about a place just like this. I will tell you about them if we get out of here," Hans responded to DJ's question. Hans felt his gut churning.

Inside the cage was a creature with the head of a bird, the body of a bull and wings. DJ noticed that it had hooves made of gold but it was not moving and they could not tell whether it was alive. DJ's heart was racing. He did not know why, but it felt like he had some kind of connection with it beyond his dream. It felt as though the prisoner were asking for their help.

The bubble began to move again. The boys tried to ascertain where they were, but before they could come up with a plausible answer, a fish appeared followed by other sea creatures. They were ugly and scary and drab looking. The boys realized they were under water. The water was so murky that it was difficult to distinguish exactly what these creatures were.

All of a sudden, the ugliest and biggest octopus they had ever seen appeared out of the murkiness and began to stretch one of its blood-red limbs toward them. Its eyes were fierce and looked right at them. The boys were terrified. Hans and DJ started to debate how to get back on solid ground while the octopus kept coming closer. The frightening tentacles were about to reach for them when Hans came up with the bright idea to grab the crown on DJ's head because it had initiated this nightmare in the first place. Immediately, the bubble that was transporting them flew upward at lightning speed.

They found themselves exactly where they were before—back on the dock. Hans still had his arms raised, holding the crown-like object above DJ's head. A beautiful glow was radiating from it. Hans lowered his arms and they stared at the fascinating object in disbelief. The shell of the oyster opened and a beautiful magical color emanated from inside as two objects emerged and floated in front of them. Then, a ghostly image appeared, instructed each of them to accept one of the objects with their right hand, and demonstrated how to do it. They automatically obliged. Then, the ghostly shadow, the oyster shell, and the magnificent glow vanished.

The boys both looked down at the objects in the palms of their hands. DJ was holding a blue pearl and Hans was holding a whitish pearl. They looked at each other, amazed at what had happened. Then they realized that they had disappeared for some time, but they did not know how long. Hans' wristwatch had stopped at 12:00 midnight.

There was no one else left on the dock, or on the adjacent beach. DJ saw the lights from the great room of the main house. The beautiful moon was still shining but the logs on the fire had begun to fade. He wondered how long they had been gone. He signaled to Hans that they should return to the house. They had a lot to tell the others. This time DJ had a witness. He smiled a victorious grin. His visions were reality, even if that reality occurred in another world.

They raced to the main house, full of excitement and hard-to-express feelings. The events that they had experienced that night were overwhelming for both of them.

— 10 —

The Shamanistic Initiatory Crisis

Grandpa and Lola had gathered everyone who was present when the boys had disappeared, into the great room. Lola gestured to one of the help and gave instructions. The rest of the household staff came to her one by one and after receiving instructions, they positioned themselves in various locations around the complex. A couple of them kept watch from the veranda while others patrolled the grounds surrounding the house.

At the girls' cottage, the commotion caught their attention. They decided to find out what was going on. Farrah and Venus led the pack.

Lola spoke to the gathering. "This is not to scare anybody," she warned. She wished to enlighten everyone about what had happened to the two boys that night.

Lola explained that she came from the family of a shaman. Her great-grandmother was the only daughter and the last child of a distinguished, skillful, and remarkable shaman practitioner. He had five wives who lived in various villages. All five wives knew of his other families. He had thirty-four sons and foresaw that his demise would come with the birth of a daughter. His prediction came true when his fifth wife bore him a daughter on Good Friday in 1888. According to the family legend, his power is passed to a descendant of his choosing: the "Homo Designare" or chosen one.

"Once this person has been chosen," she said, pausing, "he or she will be called to lead the clan on a very important mission."

Both Lola and Grandpa had suspected for some time now that a member of their clan was being called to lead an important mission. All indications were that the chosen one was DJ; however, they did not know what the mission was and only DJ could lead them to find the answer.

Laura spoke softly to Alex. "Laura, what are you two whispering about?" asked Lola.

"I have something to tell. I have kept this for awhile not knowing how to tell this to anyone," she sighed and continued. "I have experienced a dream that keeps coming to me over and over again. For some strange reason, it comes when I have touched or looked at the picture of our family that hangs over the mantel in our house."

Laura recalled what she had been seeing, "The vision takes place in a location where I have never been before. There are people dancing around a bonfire to a woman's incantation or a hymn. I am singing along with her. Then I recognize the voice and I draw nearer to the woman. She is wearing the most beautiful dress I have ever seen. It is gold and purple. As I get close to her, her appearance changes and she becomes transformed into a mermaid."

"Mother, is that you?" she recalled calling her.

"Allow me to share my experience as well," said Alex. "Like Laura, I have seen this in my dreams too, many times," he began. "I blamed it on DJ's nightmares because when he had one, I had one too, in the same night."

"What did you see in your dreams, Alex?" asked Grandpa.

"A group of people have gathered in a strange place around a bonfire. When the fire grows very high, a big boar appears from nowhere. It is walking and growling. Everyone gathers around it. They are all wearing the same clothing—a long robe with a hood. They have long beards and long hair. An older man commands me to kill the boar as he hands me a dagger. The boar starts attacking me as soon as I hold the weapon in my hand. The people cheer. I can hear their chanting."

"Did you kill the boar?" asked Lola.

"Yes, the dagger becomes a sword and I strike it once, that's all," he said, bowing his head to show remorse. He touched Laura's hand

and added, "Sorry, Laura, I did not want to tell you because you already had your hands full with DJ's problems."

Looking at each other, Alex nodded to his wife. Then she said, "Alex and I would like to share something with all of you regarding DJ as well." They tried to explain to everyone about DJ's recent troubles, the images that had been tormenting him, his loss of concentration and the incident at the hockey rink.

"He was experiencing a shamanistic initiatory crisis," explained Grandpa. Then he added, "I believe that you two were, as well."

"What do you mean by that?" asked Alex.

"A rite of passage or a calling, commonly involving physical or psychological crisis," answered Lola.

"Well, that's what is going on with him! He was trying to explain to us but we could not understand. I even blamed him for my nightmares." Laura started to cry. Alex felt the guilt as well but he was afraid of what might happen next. He bowed his head and then he gave Laura an embrace and stroked her back.

"Mom, is my experience enough to be called an initiatory crisis?" Laura asked.

"The bonfire symbolizes a gathering or a calling. The rituals of singing and incantations are the signs." She explained while pacing back and forth.

"As for Alex's dream of a bonfire and a boar, to me, it is a sign of gathering for this special mission. The boar symbolizes war. We don't know what kind of war we are facing here," Grandpa added.

"Now we know why DJ was acting so strangely," concluded Grandpa. He turned to Hans' parents and asked, "Fritz, Carmelita, has Hans experienced some initiatory crisis, too?"

Fritz replied, "I believe so. Sometimes he imagines he's a knight, but perhaps it would be better to hear it from him."

"I agree with you, Fritz. Do not worry. He will be fine. He was chosen to work with DJ on this mission, whatever it may be," answered Grandpa.

As Lola and Grandpa listened to everyone's dreams, they tried to decipher the meanings. Some got excited and some began to worry. Grandpa was confident that, since everyone in the family had experienced a vivid dream or vision that had to do with this gathering, they would all work together on a special mission.

There was momentary silence and then whispering. Lola admitted that she and Grandpa possessed the power; however, they had never been on a special mission.

"This calling is telling me that this mission is very crucial," she exclaimed. Grandpa just nodded a confirmation of agreement with his wife.

They explained that the people that worked as their household help were actually Malipayon warriors. They were known for their kindness, strength, bravery, compassion, intelligence, dedication, passion, inner beauty, high spirits and, above all, for their cheerfulness. These characteristics were the essence of their power and the values that defined the Malipayon.

There were many questions asked by Lola's children; one of them was, "What exactly does a shaman do?"

"A shaman is a person who acts as intermediary between our natural world and the supernatural world. The word shaman means 'the one who knows.' He or she is capable of entering supernatural realms to seek answers for humans and acquire knowledge to help humanity. A shaman can express these answers in many ways: verbally, musically, artistically, and in dance with special garments."

"Are we witches, too?" asked Carmelita.

"No, my dear," replied Lola. "People might call us quack doctors or faith healers, but we are none of those things. We are not witches, either. It is claimed that shamanistic practices date back before organized religions to the Paleolithic and to Neolithic eras," answered Lola. "There is not enough time tonight to explain all of this to you, but we can discuss this further in the morning," she continued. Then one of the warriors gestured a sign of good news to Lola and Grandpa who immediately understood the signal and relayed the good news to the others.

They stood up as one, and held their breath in anticipation. The door flew wide open. DJ and Hans stepped in and announced in unison, "We're back!"

With a collective sigh of relief, they all embraced each other. It was a very emotional moment marked by simultaneous laughter and tears.

Grandpa asked everyone to sit down and listen carefully without interruption to what the boys had to say. With great excitement, DJ and Hans told them everything they had experienced. Lola explained the significance of each event or object described by the boys. They concluded that these signs confirmed that today, on his fifteenth birthday, DJ was the chosen one, but that Hans played an important role. He was to guard the chosen one and would always be his right-hand man, his knight.

From Hans and DJ's account of the ogres, their description of the prisoner, and DJ's feeling of being called to free the prisoner, Grandpa and Lola concluded that the mission of the Malipayon warrior clan was to free the prisoner and restore him back to health.

It was after 1:00 AM and Grandpa called off the day. Before he and Lola said goodnight to everyone, however, Grandpa asked that all the adults, including everyone over the age of thirteen, be in the dining area for breakfast at 6:00 AM sharp. They had a mission to accomplish.

— 11 —
The Raging Whirlpool Trap

In the early hours of the morning, the moon was still watching the island of El Nido, especially the Malipayon Cove. It shone a full happy glow. They had all gone to bed exhausted by the excitement of the day—all, that is, except Lola, Grandpa, and a few of the warriors who lingered to watch over the island for any intruders.

The boys' cottage had three bedrooms, a bathroom, and a good-sized living room to share. That first night, all six of them agreed to sleep on the floor in the living room. There was a feeling of excitement among them and the energy was electric. Their strong bond as a family truly proved that they were "Malipayon." After his cousins fell asleep, DJ snuck out to show Grandpa and Lola his Librita and told them how he had acquired the book at the Our Lady Immaculate Church back in Canada. The elders told DJ that they would like to discuss the magic book with him in the morning.

"Do as you were told and keep it always with you," Grandpa said. DJ nodded and went back to the cottage with the rest of his cousins.

That night his dream was peaceful. He dreamt that he and Hans kayaked to one of the other islands. It had a cove with a narrow opening that only a small dinghy or kayak could fit through. Interestingly, thick lime corals with striking colours surrounded the lagoon. Hans commented that it might be the remains of an inactive volcano from a long time ago. DJ jumped into the water and swam. Hans could not resist the invitation of the sparkling water, so he joined in with DJ. Beautiful birds were singing. Their laughter echoed in the air like voices of angels.

Hans, on the other hand, was full of a mixture of emotions. Images raced through his thoughts and he had a restless sleep. He would have some questions for Lola in the morning. Aboud, Joshua, Takanori, and Sammi wondered what would be their role in this mission.

Inside the girls' cottage, they also slept in their living room. "This is a very special reunion," said Nadia. The other five girls were beaming in agreement. They all had pleasant dreams.

As soon as Lola and Grandpa's family parted to rest that evening, something happened that the people of the small town of El Nido would never forget. The fishermen were on their way back to the shore to call it a night. Although they were very tired, they were also cheerful because they had caught plenty of fish to sell at the market in the morning.

About a kilometer away from the shore, their small fishing boats began to spin in a gigantic whirlpool. No matter what they tried, the small motor boats did not have enough power to get out of the spiral. They kept spinning faster and faster as they were drawn to the interior of the spiral. They were trapped. The fishermen could not understand what was happening. They had never experienced such an event before. One man fell off one of the boats and quickly vanished. The others looked for him but were unable to see him as they kept spinning in the raging water.

"HELP!" they shouted at the top of their lungs.

The Malipayon warriors, who had been standing watch during the night, paid very close attention to natural occurrences and functions of nature. Their acute senses were in tune with their surroundings and they were trained to recognize even the slightest unnatural event. That night, one of the warriors was watching the edge of the water from shore and noticed that the constant lapping of the water had suddenly changed its pace and intensity. He called to his companion and alerted him to the change. They stood at the water's edge, smelled the air, listened for unusual sounds and watched for unusual lights or activity. They anticipated that something out of the ordinary was about to occur when they heard the distant voices of the fishermen calling for help.

Without hesitation, one of them ran to Grandpa and Lola who were giving instructions to the other warriors on the balcony.

"We have a visitor." This was the warrior's code for supernatural being.

"How serious is this?" Lola asked, while looking at Grandpa's face.

"We shall see," he answered.

"Those of you who are assigned to watch the cove, stay alert and keep it safe. Everyone else, let's go!" she ordered. The warriors rushed to the shore.

Grandpa wore his brown vest made of very powerful materials. His belt holstered a dagger that had been passed down to him by his ancestors. It was made of ivory from an extinct wild animal of Borneo. He took his sombrero made of vines from the rain forest and spun it into the air like a Frisbee. The hat grew until it was big enough for a couple of people to sit on. When it tipped on its side, he jumped in and flew away.

Meanwhile, Lola wore a special bandana and her enchanted *patadyong*, or robe. Around her waist she wore a magical *libon* or pouch from which she pulled another interesting object that was rolled up like a scroll called a *banig*. She unrolled it to a twelve-inch square mat woven with of sea grasses. She fluffed it up and it kept getting wider until it was wide enough for a person to sit on. When she was ready, she snapped her fingers and the enchanted *banig* swept her from the ground and flew away into the night.

Each warrior followed behind her, flying on a *baston*, a magical stick made from various woods or roots of the rainforest. It was a beautiful clear night, but Grandpa's mystical incantation made a fog appear in an instant. They did not wish to be so visible to ordinary human beings and the fog did not hinder them.

Meanwhile, the distressed fishermen held little hope of surviving the spinning whirlpool. Sopping wet from the sea spray, they clung to their boats and prayed. When the fog enveloped them, they were completely at the mercy of nature—or was it the unnatural?

The Malipayon warriors did not hesitate to dive into the fog. They lifted the fishermen off their boats one by one and brought them safely to shore. Lola used her magic *libon* to locate the fisherman that had fallen into the ocean. She swooped down on her flying *banig* and plucked him out of the whirling turbulent water. Grandpa and another warrior used the magic sombrero to salvage the night's catch. They pulled the net full of fish out of the whirlpool and dropped it on the nearest shore.

The poor and frightened fishermen sat stunned on the beach and tried to catch their breath from the ordeal. Then, realizing that they had all been saved, they embraced each other. They were so glad to be alive. They wondered who had rescued them from that freakish occurrence. Before they had a chance to thank their rescuers, they had all vanished in a fog.

Joyful to be alive, the fishermen rushed to the nearest house of the fishing village and woke up the occupants. The barking of neighborhood dogs could be heard everywhere. Soon everyone came out with lanterns to see why there was so much commotion. They gathered around the agitated fishermen who told the awesome story of their ordeal.

"Over here!" shouted one of the villagers who stood at the shoreline straining in the dark to see the whirlpool himself. He could not see the whirlpool, but he pointed to the dark ghostly shadows of the deserted fishing boats that were floating slowly toward their direction.

The fishermen rushed into the water to grab the lines of their boats. The boats were their means of earning a livelihood and were imperative to their survival. When they inspected their vessels, they could hardly believe that there was no damage to the hulls at all. Even the motors started with no problem. Only a few oars, some equipment, and supplies had floated away. Although they were relieved to have their boats back, they were fearful that another whirlpool may trap them on their next night of fishing and they may not be so lucky to escape with their lives.

Fear gripped the small fishing community. The following morning, news spread throughout the island town of El Nido about the ordeal of the fishermen during the night. Rumors circulated about the devil in the ocean. Some spoke of it in a whisper, afraid that the evil spirit would appear because it was Holy Friday. Some believers were convinced that the sea was empathetic because Jesus had died on that day according to Christian religious history. Others believed that no being could protect them from such a disaster. Nobody wanted to go anywhere near the ocean.

One of the warriors stood among the crowd and listened to what the islanders were saying about the frightening events of the night. Back in Malipayon Cove, he reported to Grandpa and Lola and the other warriors who had gathered to assess what could have caused that mysterious whirlpool.

— 12 —

Secrets of the Crystal Cave

In Malipayon Cove, an alarm clock was not necessary. The rooster crowed at five in the morning. Some were enthusiastic about getting up and others were slow. After a reminder of their mysterious task for the day, they all perked up and got ready for an early swim in the ocean, but they received instructions not to do so. Some of them were very disappointed but realized that there must be a reason, especially after what had happened to DJ and Hans the night before. They swam in the pool instead.

The water in the pool felt warm and refreshing on that early March morning, the Holy Friday of Easter. One by one, they rinsed themselves under the shower in the swimming pool area and went to their rooms to change into something comfortable. They had been instructed not to wear a wristwatch or to bring any electronic device with them. Excited by the mystery and energized by anticipation of the unknown, they were eager to tackle the day. Something told them that this would be more than an early Easter egg hunt. Some members of the family were not practicing Christians but did not protest to their in-laws' Easter celebration.

At exactly 6:00 AM, they were ready for breakfast. They were each served two boiled eggs on a bed of boiled rice with three slices of tomato, goat's milk, and a choice of fruit: banana, pineapple, mango, or papaya.

After breakfast, Grandpa told them what had transpired during the night as they were sleeping. He described the ordeal of the fishermen that the boys had met the night before. They were all very concerned, especially the boys because they considered them to be new friends.

"Are they okay?" Hans blurted.

"Yes, they have all survived," Lola answered.

"I think it has something to do with what's going on down there," Grandpa pointed to the ocean.

"Let's get our act together and move quickly. Time is running out," added DJ.

They all gathered. The children that were younger than thirteen remained at the complex in the care of some of the warriors. Parents were reassured not to worry about their younger children who seemed comfortable, playing with each other and their new guardians.

Participating in this mission with Lola and Grandpa would be their twelve children and their twelve spouses, the twelve grandchildren over age thirteen, and twelve of the warriors—fifty people. They swarmed toward the foot of the limestone mountain, Grandpa and Lola leading the pack.

Lola was a petite woman, barely standing five feet tall and about forty kilos. She had long grey hair, black eyes, and light brown complexion. At age seventy-eight, she was a strong swimmer, still able to climb trees and over mountain rocks, ride buffalos, ride horses, and play *arnis*, a Filipino martial art. She had the energy of a thirty-year-old. She was very cheerful. On that special occasion, she wore her traditional outfit: a colorful pleated *patadyong* with burgundy, deep blue, purple, and gold on the hem. She wore her unusual necklace that was made of a combination of beads and seashells with a precious gem. In her hair, she wore the most spectacular comb. The comb was an heirloom that had been passed down to her by her shaman grandmother. It was made from the wood of a rare and special underwater tree. It was decorated with various beads and precious stones that hung all the way to her shoulder. She wore bracelets and anklets and the *libon*, her magical bag, strapped around her waist. Her sandals were made of animal skin and were a little bit pointy. Her children had never seen her like this before.

She told them that this costume was only to wear for a very special ritual or occasion.

Grandpa was ten years older than Lola. He stood about 5' 8" tall, having inherited his height from his Spanish lineage. He was lean with a little pot belly. He was calm, precise, gentle, disciplined, quick thinking, and industrious. He was a wrestler, a ball player, and a good singer. He also wore his traditional outfit, which his ancestors made for such an occasion. He wore a purple and blue turban. His vest was woven from leaves and roots that were combined with animal hairs. Under his vest, he wore a plain cream shirt and a pair of Capri shorts, which they called *salwal*. In addition to the ivory dagger, on his left side hung a carved leather scabbard that held a golden sword called a *kris*. The hilt of the sword was embossed with a lion's head, the family crest, and an adornment of precious stones. At his back was a colorful fish skin case that held his bow and arrows. After a twenty-minute walk, Grandpa signaled to halt.

"We have reached our destination," he said and asked the clan to keep silent and to follow instructions. They complied.

Lola stood in front of the rocky mountain; she did some gesturing and said a spell.

"*Blandimentu anua, hic vos dominus, sinere intare*," she chanted. Then she applied a little pressure to a large rock. It slid back behind a stone wall to reveal an enormous cave. Everyone was in awe but kept silent.

They were ushered through the entrance by the warriors who educated them on everything they saw. The cavernous interior of the mountain was spectacular! Astonishing crystal stalactites hung from the ceiling and sparkled like diamonds. Sunlight beamed down through an opening in the shape of a star in the center of the ceiling and refracted through the crystals, creating prisms of rainbow-colored lights that flashed throughout the cave. The brilliant colors were captivating.

In the center of the cave floor, there was a four-foot high solid white rock shaped like an altar called a *magna taberna*. There were some objects on top of it. On the face of it, were words inscribed in gold that read "*Sacrifico, ad Gloria Pax Mundi*" which was translated

"Sacrifice, to the Glory and Peace of the World." This was the motto of the clan. This motto was also inscribed on all the crests and shields that dominated the room. At the base of the rock altar sat an old wooden trunk. It was about four feet long by three feet deep and two feet high. It was decorated with unusual cryptic symbols that were written in gold, copper, silver, and various other metals. Grandpa explained that the metallic symbols represented energy and power. Then he led everyone to the entrance of a tunnel that was grandly marked by two rock pillars.

"This is the Tunnel of Secret History," he said proudly as the clan followed him inside. The tunnel was about seven feet high. Its walls were adorned with ancient hieroglyphic drawings and carvings. Grandpa interpreted them. Lola's ancestors were a mixture of early Chinese traders and the indigenous B'laan clan. They were natives of southern Mindanao. One of the drawings was of Lola's father who was a *datu*, which means the chief. The elaborate drawing depicted the chief wearing a *saul laki* shirt, a colorful vest, *salwal* shorts, a golden dagger on his left side and a decorated belt. He wore a red, blue, and gold striped turban and sandals.

There were many other drawings on the tunnel walls. They were depictions of each family in the clan with ancient flags, crests, or shields bearing their family names: MacDonald, Schroeder, Al Shammari, Leandros, O'Leary, Khan, Marquez, Akimura, Lakota, Mandela, and two Martinez families (Laura's two brothers). They were all surprised. Neither the children nor their spouses had known that they came from the lineage of shamans.

As they all gathered, Grandpa continued, "Before we proceed to the ritual, I would like everyone to understand that this mission is crucial and that you are all needed for this operation. Now that this secret has been revealed to you, you are all obliged to contribute to the mission. After the operation, you will have a chance to continue or to reject the challenge of the clan. Understood?" Everyone responded with a nod.

"Another thing that is most important to remember is that each of you has a connection to and reason why you became part of my family," he said, addressing his in-laws.

He continued, "We know that DJ was called upon to lead us through the mission we are about to face. Now, this might not be your moment to shine, but the time will come when your own calling will be upon us. Each one of you will have a mission to undertake at an appropriate time. Understood?" Again, they all nodded.

They left the Tunnel of Secret History and were guided back to the center of the cave. They were asked to line up by fours facing the wooden trunk and to follow instructions exactly.

— 13 —

Rituals of the Shaman Warriors

They formed a line in order from the youngest to the eldest. This time Grandpa uttered a spell and the trunk opened. An intense glow came from inside the trunk. The glow got brighter and burst into flame. Then it defused and the white smoke that followed took the form of a human figure wearing a robe and a funny-looking hat. Every time it spoke, the funnel-shaped hat wiggled and bobbled about its head, face, and back. It was quite comical, but they all stifled their laughter since it was impolite.

Upon an order given by the Smoke Spirit, a neatly folded robe emerged from inside the wooden trunk and floated right in front of the first individual. This happened repeatedly until they each had a robe. The robes, called *patadyongs*, were a type of sarong but shorter. Both men and women in Asian countries wore them. These, however, were very special *patadyongs* that had been woven by various earthly creatures with unbelievable powers, which had long disappeared and now resided in a different world. The Smoke Spirit gave instructions to receive the robes with both hands, palms upward. Then they were instructed to shake them once toward the trunk light. Magically, another object that was the size of a corn kernel emerged and floated in the air right in front of each of them. They were to receive the tiny objects by the right hand, close the hand, and reopen it. When they opened their palms, each of the newly anointed warriors of the Malipayon Clan held a different precious stone, a talisman.

Amazonian bees had woven Laura's magical *patadyong* and her stone was a garnet. Scottish Highland badgers with golden ornaments that came from highland elk had woven Alex's *patadyong* and his talisman was platinum. DJ's *patadyong* had been woven by eight ancestors from eight kinds of materials decorated by eight precious stones, and his talisman was a dark blue pearl. A Saharan Scorpion had woven Hanna's *patadyong* from an ancient Druids robe, and her stone was citrine.

Each of the others received a very special *patadyong* suitable to his or her history and character, as well. The vestments were very astonishing. It was explained to them that each talisman, a precious stone or metal, was for protection and they were shown how to use it in a crisis.

They were shown various rituals and spells and began to learn how to harness their powers. They only had a few hours to master them. Generally, the shaman traverses the Axis Mundi then enters the spirit world by effecting the transition of consciousness, falling into an ecstatic trance through meditation, magic, dance, or prayer.

Lola began to teach Hans how to use his talisman with different incantations and spells. Two warriors taught him how to use a *kris*, a dagger, and a *baston*. He acknowledged that this was not an easy task.

"It is not like performing in a theater where, if you make a mistake, it does not affect your life or the life of someone else," Hans said. "This mission is demanding a perfect performance."

"Hans, you are a quick wizard. I will tell you that," praised Lola.

"Thank you, Lola, this is for the Malipayon," he responded followed by bowing to an imaginary audience.

While the others were busy learning how to use their new talismans and how to control their newly found powers, his Grandpa summoned DJ. They went into a small tunnel. The jagged tunnel had been carved out of the rock and was difficult to stand or sit in. The most important tasks DJ had to practice were concentration, concentration, and more concentration. He had to learn to focus on an object or situation and concentrate on changing its state. He had the power but did not know how to use it. Grandpa would help him through this learning process.

It was at this time that DJ confided in his grandfather. He told him about all the strange unexplained occurrences he had experienced. His Grandpa revealed to DJ that those were the signs of his calling to be a shaman. The Book of Ancient Knowledge that he had acquired back home in Canada would be useful to this mission. DJ put his hand on the book in his pocket. He felt relieved upon receiving assurances from his grandfather that he was normal but possessed a power. He needed a master to teach him how to perform properly and there were certain guidelines to follow that he needed to learn.

Grandpa had the ability to read and get into someone's mind. He asked DJ to sit cross-legged like Buddha. It was uncomfortable for him. His Grandpa asked him to close his eyes and think of the images he had experienced from the beginning. DJ told him that he might not remember everything, but he would try. He was uneasy and distracted by the uncomfortable surface on which they were sitting. It was uneven with sharp edges that hurt his buttocks and legs. Grandpa asked him to open his eyes and explained to him how to control his mind. He had to remember that the more he thought of discomfort, the more uncomfortable it would be. He had to realize that the discomfort was partially created by his mind. He was told to counteract the situation with mind control. If it was hot, neutralize it with thoughts of cold. If it was sour or bitter, sweeten it. If hard, soften it. If rough, smooth it out. If frightened, be brave. They practiced mind over matter concentration repeatedly until he finally mastered it.

Grandpa also taught DJ about infiltration and defense. He explained how he could get to someone's mind and how to block someone who was trying to infiltrate his own mind as well. Grandpa demonstrated mind control to DJ. He spoke to DJ inside his mind.

"You are weak. Yes, you're a weak boy," he said. DJ was getting weak and tired. He felt like he needed a break from this exercise.

Then he realized what was happening. Grandpa's reverse psychology worked.

"I am strong, much stronger than you are," he replied, fighting the exhaustion.

Grandpa was confident that after DJ had mastered this exercise, he would be capable of performing this task in a crisis. Then he asked DJ to take him to the bottom of the sea in his mind. Grandpa needed to see the prisoner and to understand how to get to his location. He had to assess the situation and determine what was required to undertake this mission. Only DJ had the ability to guide him there. They had to be careful and to be right.

DJ sat facing his grandfather. They closed their eyes. With masterful concentration, they traveled together in their minds below the sea, quickly passing images of their surroundings like a fast forward movie. Then they stopped. DJ showed Grandpa the exact location of the prisoner in an area known to the undersea life as the Beyond. They were not surprised by his condition. With eyes closed, the prisoner looked as though he were dying. His wings had lost their luster. His entire body had begun to decay and his heart was only faintly beating; however, his spirit was still alive and this was the most important. He was still fighting and connecting with the two of them. He was asking for help.

Both DJ and Grandpa had the same questions in their minds: Why were they chosen to undertake this mission? Who was this creature and what connection did they have with it? DJ was excited with anticipation yet cautiously attracted to the mysteries. Was this calling from the Beyond a fatal attraction?

Grandpa and DJ talked to him through their minds using mental telepathy, but the prisoner was fading. "Who are you? Can you tell us your name?" Grandpa asked, but his question went unanswered. Instead, they heard the creature whimper, "Help."

"Yes, we will help you, we will be back to get you," they communicated.

"Be careful. There are many soldiers around," responded the prisoner. His weakened spirit declined so they could no longer hear his fading voice.

Grandpa inspected the area to assess the situation and determine the best method to rescue the prisoner. After some calculation, he concluded what weapons and materials they required and how fast they needed to accomplish their mission. He glanced at DJ who had been observing every move he made. Grandpa signaled DJ to move fast before the moon changed or this mission would never happen. They only had a few hours left. He had to come up with a plan.

When they returned to their conscious level, Grandpa gathered the clan.

The warriors prepared the weapons and other items that Grandpa had determined were required for this assignment. Julio asked the family to follow him to another cave for one last ritual. The ancient rituals and ceremonies for training new recruits, taught them how to overcome adversity.

It was about a three-minute walk to get to a twin cave. The cave seemed to be about fifty feet high and about sixty feet in diameter. Although it was not as spectacular as the other cave, it was very unusual. Hundreds of roots, big and small, rooted an enormous tree at the center of the cave. Some of the roots were bigger than the torso of a human being. The roots seemed to have a mind of their own and formed ladders on both sides of the tree that reached upward in a pyramid shape. Someone asked what it was. Julio explained to them that it was a ceiba tree and that Mayans believed that it was the tree of life. The tree was about two hundred years old. It had grown through the hole in the cave ceiling as its limbs reached for the sunlight. It canopied the top of the cave outside.

They came upon an area of the cave floor that was about twelve feet long by three feet wide where burning embers glowed among pieces of broken glass. Their participation in this last ritual indicated an affirmation that they were indeed Malipayon warriors. They were shown how to use their magic to walk over the obstacle and not feel any pain or incur any injury. Each novice warrior followed and crossed the Axis Mundi into the realm of the supernatural world. They felt the ecstasy of being a shaman warrior and were ready for whatever combat they might encounter.

Before proceeding on their quest, they needed nourishment to keep up their strength and vitality. Lola invited them to sit at a beautiful crystal table shaped like a bowl. Crystal dragon feet that could rotate in all directions supported the heavy, solid, hand-cut crystal base of the table. A silver dome topped the glistening table. Lola commanded the table to serve and the silver lid retracted like the dome of the Rogers Centre retracts for a Toronto Blue Jays game. Inside, lined up perfectly were fifty little kernels. Each of them received one kernel. Lola explained to them that the food they were about to eat was from the fruit and other parts of the ceiba tree. She told them to concentrate their thoughts on a meal that they loved to eat as they were eating the kernel.

DJ thought this was an interesting way to celebrate a fifteenth birthday. Grandpa asked everyone to give him their best wishes through their minds. Then he shouted a toast, "To DJ!"

Everybody repeated in unison, "To DJ!" and his name echoed through the cave. Then they began to eat. It was a bizarre experience. Each of them ate the kernel, but amazingly, it became and tasted exactly like the complete meal on which they had been concentrating their thoughts.

"…a team of ten seahorses pulling a seashell carriage approached them. Inside was the officer. She was a beautiful mermaid…"

— 14 —

Quest for the Coral Palace

Grandpa and Lola instructed DJ and Hans to go into the depths of the ocean to look for the Mother Pearl. Their assignment was to ask her grace for the red-orange pearl, which was required to heal the prisoner if the rescue mission was successful. It had to be safely in the cave before they could begin their mission to save the prisoner. Hanna persuaded Lola to let her join DJ and Hans. Her power was so intense that she needed to use it somehow.

They wasted no time. They drifted away and in a flash, they were swimming in the ocean. With their powers, they were able to breathe like fish. Once under water, they looked around to find a sea creature that could help them find the way to the Coral Palace. They came upon a hermit crab, but it was reluctant to see them. Hans approached a barracuda who informed them that it was a long journey. Unfortunately, he could not escort them there because he was going in the opposite direction; however, he gave them directions and warned them to be careful of the deadly shells and poisonous jellyfish that lurked among the coral. He also warned them to be wary of the spiny sea urchins and electric eels that skulked behind the rocks. They thanked him and swam in the direction he pointed.

Soon they came upon a gallop of seahorses in a field of seaweed. They seemed very friendly and nodded as they approached. They explained their task to the seahorses. They were sympathetic and agreed to take them to the Coral Palace. They hopped onto the backs of the seahorses and off they sped. They travelled past many corals of different colors, shapes, and textures and some seaweed that was as large as trees. They saw many species of colorful fish and other delightful creatures. The entire underwater realm of the reef was very fascinating to the visitors from the world above. If it had not been for the urgency of their mission, they would surely have enjoyed the trip even more, taking time to explore this new environment.

Without warning, the seahorses came to an abrupt stop and skirted behind a blue coral. They explained to their passengers that a group of unfriendly-looking sharks was blocking their direct route to the Coral Palace up ahead. They all peeked between the arms of the blue coral and silently observed about twenty frenzied sharks feeding on some unlucky creature.

"Unfortunately, we must take a detour around Little Spout," said one.

"What or who is Little Spout?" asked Hanna.

"Little Spout is a volcano," it replied.

The riders again mounted the seahorses and off they veered to the right. Soon they came to an enormous underwater mountain with bubbles and steam rising from a hydrothermal vent. A small stream of lava was pouring from the summit down a pathway on one flank of the underwater volcano. The lava seemed to cool off and harden near the base of the mountain with the ocean current, but in the process, the current heated up and the visitors got very warm.

"Little Spout, I presume," said DJ. The seahorses nodded.

"Wow!" said Hans. "If that's Little Spout, I would hate to meet Big Spout."

They continued on their way around Little Spout with no incident and eventually, the kind seahorses delivered them safely to the gate of the palace. Tall, thick, blue coral surrounded the Coral Palace, and it was well guarded.

"We sincerely thank you for your help," DJ said to the seahorses.

"You are welcome, my friends. Our paths might cross again," replied the orange one.

"We wish you well with your quest," added the blue one. They swam away into distant waters until they were no longer visible.

At the gated entrance to the Coral Palace, the three visitors announced their arrival into a shell shaped like a horn. Half a dozen guards suddenly appeared from three directions. The principal guard asked them why they were there and what business they were bringing. DJ explained their intentions. He said that they must find Mother Pearl, the Queen Margarita of the Sulu Sea.

The guards were male nymph. They were very protective of the palace and adamant not to let anyone within its gates. They especially did not want humans in their territory. It was a good thing that Hanna had come along. She used her power to enchant the leader of the guard to trust them. Still, even with her powers, it was not easy to convince the guard to allow them inside the gates. They were viewed as intruders and were obliged to undergo a major scrutiny. The leader of the guard used his shell phone attached to a spider web that ran the communication network within the palace to consult an officer for further assessment.

After a brief phone conversation, the visitors were ushered just inside the gate of the Coral Palace. Here they saw an amazing structure of magnificent colors constructed of giant shells stacked one on top of the other that towered over the reef. There were more than a dozen humungous conch shells erected in this colony. It was a fantastic sight. Blue, mauve, and yellow tri-colour coral surrounded the palace.

As they were standing in awe, a team of ten seahorses pulling a seashell carriage approached them. Inside was the officer. She was a beautiful mermaid with long black hair and a band on her arm. She smiled at them and invited them to follow her to the visitors' palace.

They got on the three seahorses that stood before them and followed the carriage. Close behind them followed a battalion of nymph guards, watching intently. They were ushered to an immaculate receiving area. The three waited to meet with the queen's adviser, a yellow tortoise. They paid their respects and DJ proceeded to explain their intentions.

"Hmmm…" the tortoise said slowly, contemplating the situation. Then he added slowly and deliberately, "Let me talk to the queen first." One of the guards blew a shell horn whereupon a stingray appeared, floated under the tortoise, and whisked it away.

The Coral Queen was a beautiful mermaid with long black curly hair that draped down the front of her chest to her waist. She wore a majestic crown and held a scepter in her hand as she sat on her throne. Servants were entertaining her with music when the tortoise and stingray appeared inside her quarters. She signaled to stop the music and the slow-moving tortoise stepped off the stingray, came forward and bowed his head before the queen.

"Three humans have entered your reefdom, your Majesty. If it please your Majesty, they are asking for your wisdom and generosity in the hope that you will be able to help them see the Mother Pearl, Queen Margarita," he said eloquently.

The Coral Queen instructed one of the spider guards to show her these humans. In a few seconds, the spider guard produced an image of the three visitors on his web. "Ask the guard to send them here," she commanded.

At the visitors' palace, the guard in charge received instructions on his shell phone to let the visitors proceed to the queen's quarters. Then he blew his shell horn and three stingrays scooped the visitors away. They enjoyed the flight. The stingrays were careful not to drop them because the coral below had very sharp edges. After a few loops around some shell structures, they entered the queen's coral quarters. The surroundings were magnificent. DJ, Hans, and Hanna paid homage to the mermaid queen and she welcomed them. They noticed that the tortoise was sitting on her right hand side. A female jellyfish with a colorful hat was floating behind the queen. Hanna thought she might be the queen's secretary. She was fascinated by the variety of creatures that lived in the ocean. Then she saw a group of young mermaids, who appeared to be about her own age, giggling and whispering. They reminded her of her own friends in her world.

"What brings you here, humans?" the queen queried.

"Your highness, your gracious queen of the Sulu Sea Reef, we have a very important task to accomplish that involves the rescue of a prisoner who is being held captive by the sea ogres that live below the western reach of your reefdom," DJ explained.

There was a frightful gasp from all the attendants in the room. The tortoise retreated inside his shell. The queen sat back on her throne, then leaned forward and gestured DJ, Hans, and Hanna to come closer. The queen suggested that they whisper so that no one else, especially the gossip fish or spy serpents, could hear their plan. When they had finished explaining, the queen asked the servants to prepare her carriage. Soon they were on their way, riding with the queen in her carriage escorted by nymph guards and attendants.

— 15 —

The Search for the Healing Pearl

The Coral Queen was the prime guardian of Mother Pearl, who resided in a hidden cave. Extraordinary, huge, blue-green coral swayed in the current to camouflage the cave's entrance. Although the palace of the Coral Queen was not far from Mother Pearl's cave, she never disturbed her unless it was for a very important and special request.

"Mother Pearl is kind and generous," she explained to her guests, "but she can also have a temper. You cannot wake her up on a certain day, at a particular time, because you will be greeted by the wrath of the ocean."

The entrance to Mother Pearl's cave was in the form of an oyster shell. It sparkled in pink, blue, yellow, and silver hues as streams of sunlight seeped through the water, danced among the blue-green coral, and landed on the shell doors.

"In order to be granted an audience with Mother Pearl," explained the Coral Queen to her guests, "a special ritual must be performed that involves dozens of creatures." She went on to explain that, in order for Mother Pearl to be in good humor when she was awakened, the Coral Queen must sing a particular song that only she, and no one else, could sing and the sea harp must accompany her voice in perfect tune.

"If Mother Pearl is pleased by the sound, the opening oyster shell entrance will glow," she said. "If she is not satisfied, watch out for smoke that will puff from the oyster shell. It can be blinding, as has been demonstrated hundreds of times before."

The Coral Queen really wanted to help DJ, Hans, and Hanna. She understood the enormity of their mission. She cleared her throat and gestured to the harpists to begin. A school of striped angelfish began to pluck the sea harp in an unusual melodic sequence and made the instrument vibrate an enchanting tune. The cheerful sound resonated in the waves and the visitors were astounded. The Coral Queen began to sing with the most beautiful sweet voice that they had ever heard. She had the voice of an angel and sang her melody from the heart. A chorus of yellow-tailed blue damselfish accompanied her in perfect harmony while golden butterfly fish fluttered and danced creating the rhythm.

When she had finished singing her magnificent song, the entire entourage held its breath in anticipation of Mother Pearl's response. Slowly, the oyster shell entrance opened with a faint glow that got brighter until it became the most brilliant light they had ever seen. All who were present, human, and every other living creature, had to cover their eyes. Then the glow faded and sparkling bubbles began to emerge. There, in the background, the Mother Pearl stretched up her arms and yawned. Smiling, she sat up on her throne, clapped her shells and announced that that was the best vocal song she had heard in a hundred years. The entire entourage breathed a collective sigh of relief and all the creatures chatted happily to each other in their excitement.

"Why have you awakened me, Coral Queen?" she asked.

"Mother Pearl, with all your radiance, beauty and kindness, these young humans have come to ask a favor of you. If you will allow, I will bid them come closer to you," said the Coral Queen.

Upon a gesture from Mother Pearl to proceed, DJ, Hanna, and Hans stepped forward and knelt before her with heads bowed down.

"Rise up, and plead your case," she said. They stood up and DJ explained about their plans to rescue the prisoner.

"Your Majesty," he began. "We have been called upon, as Malipayon warriors, to rescue a prisoner being held captive in the deepest ocean chasm of the Sulu Sea by a swarm of ogres and evil creatures. The prisoner is very weak and dying. If we are successful in our attempt to free him from the stone prison and bring him back to our world, we will require a certain red-orange pearl with magical healing properties in order to heal his body. This red-orange pearl only exists in your possession."

As soon as she heard what they intended to do, Mother Pearl was perturbed. She seemed deep in thought as deep furrows creased her brow. The entourage again held its collective breath, awaiting a response from Mother Pearl. Suddenly, the look of concern on her face turned into a valiant one.

She stood up in front of them and boldly announced, "The time has come. I have been sleeping here in my cave for thousands of years hoping that one day, when I awoke, I would hear someone speak the words I have just heard."

Then she paced back and forth and continued. "The west territory has been condemned for thousands of years. The time for deliverance has surely arrived. With my full blessings, I will give you all my strength, power, and even my life to rescue the poor..." She stopped, then composed herself again and continued. "Free him from the hands of the sea monsters and change the entire ocean forever!" The crowd bowed their heads and gave the three visitors their blessings, as well. It was so quiet that even the live coral paused in their swaying movement.

Mother Pearl welcomed them all into her enormous cave but only DJ, Hans, and Hanna were allowed to enter another interior cave where the pearls were stored. The three human visitors were amazed by the tons and tons of pearls that ranged in size from small grains to large beach balls. They glowed spectacular shades of green, blue, yellow, pink, black, and white; however, they did not see a red-orange pearl anywhere. Finding the one they needed among the millions they saw seemed to be an impossible task. Surely, it would take years to be able to find, but they needed it now—a life was at stake!

The urgency of their mission pressed on their minds and DJ could hear Grandpa's voice telling him to concentrate. He did not want to waste any time. He immediately touched his right side pocket and felt the Librita. He took it out and rubbed the center of the book and it grew to a normal size. DJ gently pushed aside some pearls to clear a space in the middle of the cave floor. He calmly sat down. Legs crossed like Buddha he took a deep breath, closed his eyes, placed the palm of his hand on the book and concentrated. Then he spoke to the book while Hans and Hanna stood by anxiously waiting for what would happen next. They had great faith in DJ, gave him their full support as leader, and did not question his actions.

"From every letter that is written, your ancient knowledge is freely given. Tell me in this undersea world, how to find the healing pearl," he said. Immediately, the book opened flat to a page somewhere near the middle.

With his eyes still closed, DJ concentrated on the mystical hieroglyphics and characters inscribed in the book. Images and directions on a map in the book became clear to him. On the map in the book, he located the spot in which they were standing in the cave.

Then he applied what Grandpa had taught him. "When something is difficult, concentrate and you will find the solution," Grandpa's words infiltrated his mind.

His mind concentrated on the piles and piles of pearls that surrounded them. Some were stacked unsafely as high as the cave ceiling. He began to picture a path to the red-orange pearl the shaman way. As he saw the way to the pearl in his mind, he gave instructions to Hans and Hanna to walk this way and that, climb here and look behind there.

"Move to your right, Hans, and hold back that big blue one to keep the pile from falling," he said. Hans followed his instructions.

"Hanna, climb onto the huge pink pearl on top of the one that Hans is holding back and look behind the middle-sized pale green one, about the size of a softball," he instructed.

Hanna had some difficulty climbing the smooth slippery pearls but managed to get to the spot that DJ had indicated. She spotted a middle-sized pale green pearl, looked behind it, and squealed with triumphant delight.

"We found it!"

Finally, they emerged from the mouth of the interior cave and DJ showed the waiting crowd what he held in his hand. The crowd cheered at the sight of the golf-ball-sized, red-orange pearl.

Mother Pearl and the Coral Queen were waiting for them with their entourage. Mother Pearl handed him a special pouch in which to carry the precious object. DJ thanked the entire reefdom for their generosity. As a token of remembrance, he left them his miniature puck with a maple leaf design that he had found in his pocket while reaching for the Librita. The stingrays were ordered to take them back to shore. In a split second they were back again in the cave with Grandpa and the rest of the clan.

This part of their mission was accomplished. Lola received the pouch with care and kept it in a safe place. Hanna greeted her mom and dad, who patted her head and embraced her, saying, "We are very proud of you."

— 16—

The Deadly Perils of Jolo

Grandpa explained to the Malipayon warriors that they needed to accomplish one more task before they could proceed with their mission to rescue the prisoner. To be able to see in the deepest darkest abyss of the Sulu Sea where the prisoner was being held captive, they needed to acquire some sacred candles that were hidden in the cave of a sea creature called Kamut Hari. He explained that he and Lola had summoned their powers of concentration to locate Kamut Hari, but for some reason, they could not. He asked DJ to sit in the center of the group while they all directed their powers to augment his.

They all complied and DJ concentrated on Kamut Hari. Then DJ abruptly interrupted his concentration, looked at Grandpa, and said, "There is a barrier that I am not able to break through." A look of alarm came over Grandpa and Lola.

"What shall we do?" Lola asked.

"The path is blocked with unidentified material or power," Grandpa explained.

Without hesitation, DJ reached for his Librita inside his pocket. He opened it up, closed his eyes, spoke a few words, and read the instructions. Then he turned and addressed the clan.

"According to the Book of Ancient Knowledge, we must procure a key to the gateway of Kamut Hari's reefdom from the Keeper of the Keys," he announced.

Speaking not with words but through their minds, he commanded that they follow him using their magic power of concentration. They found themselves on the sandy shore of a small but long island, one of a hundred and fifty islands in this archipelago. DJ told the confused clan that they were on the island of Jolo of the Sulu Archipelago.

Beyond the sand, there were a few huts quietly standing in the shade of gracefully swaying palm trees. No other humans were visible. It was as though the island were deserted. A strange feeling came over them and they remained alert to any unusual signs or events. Grandpa took a deep breath and smelled the air. He nodded and proceeded to dig his hand into the ground. Lola and Julio examined the dirt.

"Secure," she said, with a nod. Lastly, the patriarch of the clan scooped some seawater into the cup of his hand, smelled, and tasted it. Everyone watched and waited.

"Yes, it is safe," he finally concluded.

Hans, Joshua, and Aboud were assigned to inspect the waters surrounding the island. Diving into the water, the three vanished quickly. While the others waited for them to return, Grandpa told them a brief history of the island.

"Our ancient ancestors settled, traded, and lived peacefully on this island," he said. "A Chinese merchant named this island Jolo. It means good and honest people. Merchants could leave their goods on this shore unguarded and no one stole them. According to our history, crates of goods sat here for months, intact. Ninety percent of the settlers on this island are of Chinese descent. They have loved this place since that time and their descendents have been living here for over five hundred years." Grandpa concluded, "I am very puzzled that there seems to be no sign of them now."

As Grandpa spoke, DJ consulted his Librita for further instructions. He determined that, to find the Keeper of the Keys to the gateway of Kamut Hari's reefdom, where the Sacred Candles were kept, they must ascend to the summit of the sleeping volcano located five kilometers in from the shore.

The three cousins surfaced from their dive into the sea.

"I'm glad you have returned quickly. Tell us what you know," Grandpa said.

Hans, who was clearing his ear, replied, "The base of this island is something that one could never imagine. Five enormous square pillars under its perimeter and one gigantic round pillar in the center support it. They appear to be natural formations of volcanic and coral materials."

"Yeah, we can't get closer somehow. There appears to be thick water like gelatin blocking our passage for closer examination. In addition, the sulfur dioxide smell was getting stronger," added Joshua.

"Wildlife is plentiful, especially sharks and manta rays," finished Aboud.

Now that they knew what they were dealing with around and under the island, they turned their attention inland toward the dormant volcano that dominated the skyline of the island. It stood a very steep twenty-one hundred feet above sea level. A thick tropical rainforest began beyond the huts and extended to the top of the mountain.

"Big Spout, I presume," Hans said, recalling the underwater volcano they had encountered during their last task.

DJ explained their situation according to the Book of Ancient Knowledge.

"The Keeper of the Keys lives deep inside the volcano. We must descend from the volcano's rim to find him. There are a couple of major paths leading to the summit. Dangerous obstacles created by supernatural powers block all of these paths. You can be trapped by deadly tarantulas, bitten by poisonous snakes, ravaged by gluttonous ants, swarmed by killer bees, or eaten by all sorts of wild beasts. Be careful with the scent as well, because it can put you to sleep and you will never wake up," he warned.

After a brief discussion, it was decided that Grandpa and Lola would attempt to reach the summit by flying on Lola's magical *banig.* Although DJ's Librita warned of invisible infrared laser rays being emitted from the center of the volcano, this seemed to be their best option. Suspicious that this seemed too easy a method to reach the summit and that it might be a trap, the others were instructed to wait at the base of the mountain for their report.

Lola took her small *banig* from inside her magical *libon*. She unraveled it and waved it up in the air. It spread wider and the patriarch and the matriarch of the clan stood side by side, while the magical *banig* wrapped around them up to their heads. Then it picked them up and flew like a stick that disappeared into the air.

As the Malipayon warriors concentrated their powers on their flight, they could see hundreds of normally invisible infrared laser rays beaming in many directions like spotlights crisscrossing the sky. Had these been ordinary spotlights, this would have been a great light show to watch; however, laser lights were potentially deadly. They watched as Lola and Grandpa dodged this way and that to avoid the deadly rays, but they were not able to find a clear pathway to the summit of the mountain.

Suddenly, they were captured in the grip of one of the laser rays. They were frozen in midair and unable to move.

The warriors below were stunned and did not know what to do, but DJ was quick thinking and ordered his Librita to open in preparation for a flight. Then he ordered the others to stay behind and nudged Hans' arm.

"Come on! Let's go," he shouted. They jumped on the Librita and sped quickly to the site of their captured grandparents.

They approached with caution, being careful not to be captured themselves. They were able to avoid the other laser beams but needed to keep moving. DJ commanded the Librita to maneuver safely around their grandparents avoiding the lasers. Then DJ closed his eyes and called to Hans.

"Concentrate!" he shouted above the noise of the turbulence created by the wild lasers.

With DJ and Hans projecting their full powers of concentration on their grandparents and their grandparents projecting their full powers of concentration from within the laser, they were able to break its hold. As soon as they were released, Grandpa and Lola sped back down to the base of the mountain followed by DJ and Hans.

The others had been watching with baited breath and were relieved that they were unhurt by the ordeal.

They wasted no time. There was work to be done. Although it seemed as though all this preparation for the rescue was taking a long time, within the realms of the real world, only a few moments had passed.

"Clearly, that did not work," said Grandpa. "We will have to go to plan B."

— 17 —

The Trek to the Summit

Plan B began with DJ consulting his Book of Ancient Knowledge to decide which would be the most direct and least treacherous pathway to the summit of the mountain.

DJ suggested that they pair up with a partner so that they could keep a better eye on each other's safety. It was decided that they should only communicate through their minds so that the sound of their voices would not alert any enemies. A few of the warriors were assigned to watch the base of the mountain for signs of supernatural interference so that they could warn the others telepathically. The rest of the Malipayon warriors followed DJ to the trailhead. Thick spiraling vines almost completely concealed the path's entrance.

Julio inspected the entrance to the pathway for signs that warriors from another clan had broken the seal or that treasure hunters had been there. Since there were no markings like cut or snapped branches or torn leaves, he concluded that no treasure hunters had taken this route to the summit. On the other hand, the seal had been broken. He pointed out that warriors from another clan in search of a talisman or medicinal herbs or roots may have broken the seal.

"One of the first rules of being a warrior," he said using his thoughts, not his voice, "is to cover your tracks and leave no trace of having been there." Then he pointed out that the pathway had been disturbed and had not been resealed. He concluded that the other warriors must have met their fate somewhere along the trail up ahead; otherwise the trail would have been resealed for their own security.

"It is certain that any warrior who climbed the trail did not return," he thought sadly.

The Malipayon warriors followed DJ and Hans cautiously up the trail two by two. The strong odor of ginger and castor oil led them to believe that perhaps the other warriors had been seeking medicinal roots. Mahogany and acacia trees dominated the forest and there were palm, red banana trees, and bamboo grasses. Beautiful foliage covered the ground but DJ warned his troupe not to deviate from the path to touch or admire the plants. The tropical sun was beating down on the sultry forest, and although they walked in the shade of the lush treed canopy, the air was very thick with humidity and it felt as if they were in a sauna.

A strong sulfurous odor began to engulf them. Their trek led them past a naked field of basalt lava with cinder cones, burping mud pots, bubbling thermal pools, and hissing fumaroles that drenched them in hot vapor. A geyser suddenly erupted beside them, a phenomenon that occurs when a huge mass of underground magma heats water to steam, which presses to the surface. Although the volcano was inactive above ground, there was no telling what was going on below.

Soon they came to a fork in the path. DJ signaled to stop while he focused his thoughts on the area to determine the best route to take. The fork to the left seemed to go straight up in the direction they were headed. The fork to the right seemed to veer slightly back down the mountain in the opposite direction.

"It can't be this obvious," he thought. He looked around for any sign that might help him decide and noticed an oddly shaped palm tree between the two forks in the trail. The tree bent downward and pointed to the right side. DJ sensed that this was a sign that they should heed. He chose the right fork in the trail. The clan followed, and once they had passed the slight dip down the mountain slope, the trail resumed its upward direction toward the summit.

Suddenly, a quail flew out of the bushes with its wings flapping loudly and feathers rustling. It startled them but they were careful not to utter a sound. DJ took it as a sign that danger lay ahead and alerted the others not to let their guard down.

Silently, he scouted past a few trees. He heard a strange sound like lips smacking and clicking jaws and slowly peeked around a bend in the trail. There in the center of the path was a swarm of thousands of killer ants, each about the size of a man's thumb. They had attacked a wild boar and brought it down in its tracks. Ravenously, they were gorging on the half-eaten carcass and did not notice DJ watching in silence. He signaled the clan with his mind and made them aware of the situation. They waited patiently until the flesh of the boar was completely devoured. It took only a few moments, and the ants moved down the mountain through the forest in search of their next meal.

They resumed their trek up the mountain, stepping over the skeletal remains of the boar, keeping silent and vigilant.

Like some of the others, Hanna kept a ready hand on the hilt of her weapon, a magical *kris* holstered in a scabbard hanging by her side. She was partnered with Julio, who walked next to her. She had faith in his honor and ability as a warrior to defend against any predators and protect her if she needed help. She hoped that she could do the same for him. The one thing she knew was that she was now a warrior, and whatever happened, she would fight to the death to defend her family. She focused on the path ahead, all her senses alert.

Soon they came upon a screen of bamboo grasses that were as tall as trees. They were woven into a specific pattern but no one could decode it.

"Is it a razor?" asked one silently with his mind.

"I think it is teeth," thought another.

"Fangs or claws," thought a third.

DJ consulted his Book of Ancient Knowledge. Just as he had surmised, it warned of deadly poisonous snakes ahead. He warned the others. They drew their weapons. The beating sound of jungle drums seemed to get louder and closer until they realized the sound was that of their hearts pounding.

Suddenly, a cobra slithered toward DJ. He reacted almost instantly and cut off its head with his magical *kris*. Seconds later, a poisonous adder attacked. This time Grandpa and Hans slashed it at the same time. Then one snake after another attacked the group from different directions. One dropped itself down from a branch above Julio's head. Hanna reacted immediately and slashed it in two before it could harm him.

Then the onslaught of assailing snakes ceased and was replaced by a steadily growing and advancing thorny vine that was slowly surrounding the warriors. They slashed and stabbed the vine but at each cut, two new shoots would grow instantly. To make matters worse, at every new slash in the vine, a toxic scent was released. DJ realized the futility of fighting the deadly vine and before it could completely engulf or suffocate them, he created an opening to the trail ahead with his mind-over-matter concentration and ordered his followers to run through to the other side. Once they had all safely passed through, he sealed the opening.

Julio and Hanna stood to the side and counted the members of the group to make sure they had all made it through. They were alarmed when they counted three extra warriors in their group. They alerted the others that three supernatural beings had infiltrated their clan and disguised themselves as three of their members. They told them to continue and pretend that they did not know.

With his powers of mental telepathy, DJ told them to use their minds to ask their partners the name of the clan. If the partner did not respond with the correct answer, they were to use their magical power to throw a net on the imposter and capture him at once.

The plan worked. The warriors discovered who the three imposters were and immediately captured them in a net that was released from their *patadyongs*. As soon as they were captured, a potion that coated the net and made them sleepy subdued the imposters. Once asleep, the imposters were transformed into their original state. They were a python, a giant black scorpion, and a komodo dragon. DJ ordered his warriors to hang the nets from a mahogany tree.

"Why can't we finish them?" someone asked.

"According to the Book of Ancient Knowledge, more creatures will appear in every drop of their blood," said DJ. They followed his instructions and hung the nets containing the captured supernatural creatures in the tree. DJ explained that, within an hour, the nets would dissolve and there would be no traces of the clan.

They continued up the steep slope. The path got narrower and they had to climb a number of boulders that obstructed the trail. It looked as though there had been a recent landslide in the area. The trail narrowed to just a foot wide. They looked down over the bluff. It was a sheer cliff with a one thousand foot drop straight down one side. A sparkling waterfall, split by a large buttress, dropped down onto a series of jagged ledges to a river far below.

They had to continue in single file and linked to each other with their magical *patadyong*s for safety. The air got thinner the higher they climbed.

Finally, they reached the summit. The volcanic crater was about five hundred feet across. The Librita cautioned them that invisible tarantula webs that had the capacity to capture intruders with a sticky substance surrounded the crater. The captured victims are injected with a paralyzing poison by a brood of tarantulas as big as a human hand that proceed to devour them alive. Because the tarantula webs were invisible, it looked as though the few human skeletons and the skeletal remains of other creatures were hanging in midair. It was a very eerie sight. The stench of rotting flesh of recently trapped creatures filled the air.

Lola reminded everyone to remain silent and keep breathing under control. With her mental powers, she concentrated on an incantation. Then Grandpa released his power to substitute the invisible tarantula web fence with a Malipayon fence. As soon as this was accomplished, the Malipayon warriors passed through to the other side of the fence and breathed with relief. They had to hurry, for this was just a temporary exchange.

— 18 —

The Keeper of the Keys to the Gateway

It was decided that Grandpa and Lola would descend into the crater first in order to disarm or neutralize the laser device that wildly scoured the sky for intruders. Some of the warriors stood guard against evil spirits while the others encircled the rim of the crater and concentrated their powers on creating luminous green laser beams of their own.

Grandpa and Lola cruised down into the heart of the crater on the magical *banig* as if it were a starship. The warriors emitted the powerful Malipayon light beams from their eyes and focused them directly on the deadly infrared beams in order to manipulate them away from Grandpa and Lola. The jagged rock interior looked foreboding. The source of the deadly infrared laser beams was somewhere deep in the darkness of the crater.

Using the *banig* for protection against the deadly beams, Grandpa and Lola followed the red rays to their source. A red cut-crystal rock was spinning, turning, and bobbing on top of a hot water fountain from a dormant lava vent. Sunlight that gleamed down to the stone was reflected to the exterior in the form of the wild infrared rays.

"What do you think?" Lola asked her husband.

"Brilliantine," he replied. "Hurry, do something!" he added.

Reaching inside her magical *libon*, Lola grabbed a black diamond and crushed it in her hand. Then she threw the black diamond dust at the base of the red brilliantine rock. She hoped the diamond particles would neutralize the effects of the red laser beams and protect the Malipayon clan. She also hoped that the supernatural residents of the crater would accept the brilliant display of sparkling black diamonds as a gesture of good will and respect.

"It's working!" said Grandpa, as they watched the deadly infrared laser beams unite with the sparkling black diamond dust. They synchronized and merged with the luminous green laser light released by the Malipayon warriors.

They were relieved that the laser was under control and waited anxiously for any sign of the crater's inhabitants. As their eyes focused into the dark recesses of the jagged crater, Lola was surprised to see an unusual creature standing silently before her. She did not know how long it had been there. The creature had the body of a tarantula spider but the head of a human female. Her hair was kinky, black, long, and draped almost to the ground. Her face showed no emotion. The three stood silently sizing each other up.

"I believe these belong to you," the spider woman finally spoke and with a gesture of her arm, DJ, Hans, and the rest of the warriors appeared. Grandpa and Lola were horrified to see that they were each wrapped securely in a silky web, unable to break free. They were escorted by huge tarantulas.

Then the spider woman commanded the tarantula guards to release them, and with one of their razor-sharp hands, they sliced the webs and freed the Malipayon warriors.

"Was it necessary to do that?" asked Lola in a commanding voice.

"Very necessary," explained the spider woman. "You are not alone. The Hunters are lurking at the summit searching for prey. We needed to bring your people inside. Follow me," she ordered.

With no argument, they all followed the spider woman. She led them through a dimly lit tunnel. It was a lava cave with very little air and a sulfurous odor. It was about a three-minute walk but the trek seemed endless. They finally arrived at a parasite cone of the dormant volcano. The only source of fresh breathable air was through the vent of the cone. A narrow beam of sunlight was piercing through the vent from outside and shone onto a rock of brilliantine, which was used to disperse light throughout the cave. There, sitting in the center of the cave below the cone, was an older man wearing plain khaki clothing and a turban wrapped around his head. His skin was tanned. He had Chinese eyes a small nose, and his beard resembled the ash of the volcano itself. He stood as the Malipayon entered. He was about five feet four inches tall and lean. Finally he spoke.

"Malipayon, why are you here?" he addressed the clan. "Are you seeking fortune, magic, or immortality?"

"Your Gracious Rajah Saleman, Keeper of the Keys, we are here before you to humbly request your permission to borrow a key to enter through the gateway to the reefdom of Kamut Hari," answered DJ.

"We have undertaken a mission that is extremely critical and that involves the rescue of the…" Grandpa hesitated, and then decided to confide, "The prisoner of the Beyond. I believe you know of whom I speak," he added.

"Ahhh…" sighed the Rajah. "No one could ever forget what happened." His thoughts seemed to drift sorrowfully to a place in his past. Then he continued.

"There have been a few attempts at his rescue but all have failed; therefore, evil spirits populate the underworld. I wish with all my heart and soul that you will succeed with this rescue mission. Many clans and warriors have been called upon throughout the ages, but all rescue attempts have concluded in dismay," he said, sadly shaking his head.

"The prisoner's condition has deteriorated of late," said Grandpa.

"We know that he is very weak and will soon die unless he is rescued and revived," added DJ. The other Malipayon warriors observed and listened reverently to the discussion among Rajah Saleman, Grandpa, and DJ.

"Very few have knowledge of Kamut Hari. He is not easy to find down there. Someday, the world will discover the truth about him," said the Rajah. Understanding the urgency of the rescue mission, he stood up, waved his hand, and the spider woman guard descended from the ceiling. He whispered to her and she disappeared. When she returned, she was carrying a basketful of spider eggs.

"Before I lend you the key," said the Rajah, "I want to give each of you a special talisman, a gift from my *Kalahari,* my tribe, please," he said, gesturing toward the basket.

Grandpa and Lola chose first and the rest followed. They were asked to drink the eggs for extra strength and power. They tasted surprisingly good. Then the Rajah told the Malipayon clan that the key they were seeking was hidden in the throat of the volcano, inside a red stone located between the double brilliantine rocks on a narrow ledge; however, his revelation came with a warning.

"Whoever will retrieve the key will have to act quickly," he cautioned. "Sometimes, the pressure from underneath will pull one downward and sometimes push one upward." When he asked which Malipayon warrior would retrieve it, DJ volunteered.

DJ was ushered to an area of the cave that had access to the throat of the crater. He stuck his head through the access. He could feel a great sucking wind pressure pulling him below. Asserting his newly augmented power acquired from drinking the tarantula eggs, he released a web that spanned the distance across the abyss and clung to the sides of the crater's throat. He understood why they had to drink this powerful talisman and was grateful.

DJ climbed onto the web. His new power kept him from sticking and he was able to maneuver on the web like the tarantulas. He looked down into the abyss and saw only darkness. A great wind pressure was sucking him downward. He held tight. Suddenly, the pressure reversed and a hurricane force wind came from below, forcing him upward in the web. He had to hold his breath, so his lungs would not fill with fine ash. This upward draft worked to his advantage, and he was able to reach the narrow ledge and grab the red stone from between the double brilliantine rocks. Then he quickly and carefully made his way back across the web to the access point where he had begun.

Back safely with the others who had been encouraging him as they watched, he handed the red stone triumphantly to the Rajah.

"You did a magnificent job," said the Rajah. "You are the first to ever retrieve this stone. You deserve to have its contents." With those words of praise, the Rajah placed the red stone in a bowl and spider woman poured a few glistening drops of liquid from a vessel.

"This is a collection of the teardrops of a nymph and a mermaid. Their homes and families were destroyed by that unforgettable conflict between different worlds," the Rajah recalled with moist eyes. They watched in reverence as the red stone melted away, disclosing a glistening crystal key.

"Here is the key to the gateway of Kamut Hari's reefdom," he said, holding the bowl toward DJ. "Make sure to use it honorably. Once you are finished with it, destroy it so that it does not fall into the hands of evil spirits."

"Thank you, your grace. We will never forget your hospitality and generosity. The Malipayon clan will forever be a friend of your *Kalahari,* your tribe," assured Grandpa.

The two elders embraced and gave their blessings to each other and the Malipayon said goodbye. The spider woman ushered them to a secret passage, which was another vent of a dormant volcanic cone.

"Come this way," she said, "and the Hunters will not find you."

They all hopped on their magical flying devices and followed DJ's command: "Straight down!" They collected the warriors that had been standing guard at the base of the mountain and flew straight to the Crystal Cave.

— 19 —

The Sacred Candles of Sulu Sea

Everyone encircled the altar. Grandpa, Lola, Hans, and DJ were inside the circle facing the altar. Grandpa had one last thing to explain to the warriors before they were to leave on their quest. He said that timing was crucial and that they must move swiftly once they had entered the realm of the supernatural.

Holding up a crystal hourglass contained in a cage made from the wood of the ceiba tree, he warned, "We must return from our mission before the sands in the upper chamber of the hourglass have completely fallen through to the bottom or we can never return again."

"Is everyone ready? Raise your hands," Grandpa instructed as he turned the hourglass upside down and set it on the altar.

Wearing their enchanted *patadyong*s, they spun around, reached out their right hands, and released their powers. Immediately, a ring of fire encircled them. As it diffused, the ray of light that remained suddenly transported them at high speed to the supernatural undersea world. In the shape of an arrow, DJ led the clan, followed by Grandpa, Lola, Hans, and the others.

This water, called the Sulu Sea, was clear. Some parts looked emerald and turquoise. Each person in the clan underwent an immediate metamorphosis and developed gills like a fish. As their respiratory systems were transformed like those of amphibians only in reverse, they were able to breathe under water.

Before they could undertake their mission to rescue the prisoner, they needed to accomplish one more task. They had to find the sacred undersea candles located somewhere in the depths of the Sulu Sea in the reefdom of Kamut Hari. Without the sacred candles, they would not be able to navigate the deep abyss where the prisoner was confined. How could they find Kamut Hari's reefdom?

Using his magical powers and his power of concentration, DJ was able to focus on Kamut Hari and he could envision him. Kamut Hari was known to be a magical water creature with a good spirit. He was friendly, but only if he liked you. This five-foot-tall being had the head of a human and the body of a dragon seahorse. His hair was prickly like a sea urchin but a little bit longer and sharper. He had six strong arms. His body was covered with colored stripes from his neck to his hips, and from his waist to tail was a kind of soft coral that curled inward. He carried a bow with him at all times and used his prickly hair as arrows for defense when threatened. The many colors of his body provided camouflage against his enemies or predators, as he appeared to be just another coral. He lived in a secret cave and guarded magical candles that no one knew about other than Rajah Saleman, Keeper of the Keys.

DJ instructed his Book of Ancient Knowledge to lead them to Kamut Hari's reefdom. Instantly, they were transported to another region of the reef. Before them was an enormous gateway that blocked the entrance to a vast secure section of the reef. DJ inserted the crystal key that they had obtained from Rajah Saleman into the ornamental silver lock that secured the gateway. It unlocked the gateway and the Malipayon clan entered into Kamut Hari's reefdom. DJ locked the gate after everyone had entered and put the key safely back into his pocket.

The clan encountered many colorful and fascinating sea creatures on its journey. On their left, a herd with dozens of seahorses glided by. Blobs of jellyfish floated on their right. Thousands of trumpet fish suddenly swarmed them. The male trumpet fish sounded their alarms to alert the colony to a possible threat. The female trumpet fish were considered the gossipers of the sea, and although they looked very beautiful, other sea creatures did not trust them. A fire urchin watched them from his resting spot on top of a pink coral. It was one of the many corals protecting the Philippine islands. It was a spectacular sight; however, the beauty of the reef was deceiving. It concealed hidden dangers that lurked in the depths of the abyss below.

It was quite a journey. Although the scenery was magnificent, the warriors did not notice it. The urgency of this crisis did not allow time for sightseeing. They were all aware of the sands of time falling through the hourglass, but they trusted their leader and followed unquestioningly.

DJ found Kamut Hari right where he had envisioned him. He was singing to the rhythm of seashells that he was tapping together with two of his six hands. Although Kamut Hari seemed to be preoccupied by his music, DJ thought it best not to make any sudden moves. He did not want to frighten him away or to confront him directly, which might force him to fight if he thought he were being attacked. Regardless of how busy Kamut Hari looked, he still had four additional hands ready for defensive combat. The clan cautiously stood its distance to avoid upsetting him.

Kamut Hari seemed to be in a good mood and he began to swim playfully through the crevices of large coral. DJ devised a plan and sent Farrah to persuade him to lead her to his cave. Farrah felt honored to be chosen to carry out this task and happy to be allowed the privilege to use her power. She appeared not far from Kamut Hari also holding shells in her hands. With an enticing smile on her beautiful face, she danced toward him, tapping her seashells in a captivating rhythm while reciting her incantation: "From the tip of my hair to the tip of my toe, I look exactly the same as you," she sang.

He stopped. In a moment of shyness, he partially hid his face behind one of the lacy green veil corals, but his gaze was fixated on her. Her beauty enchanted him. In his eyes, she looked just like him, only her body was a different color. He was attracted to her immediately.

Farrah continued to dance to the rhythm of her seashells. Soon Kamut Hari emerged from his cover. Fascinated by her performance, he tried to imitate her. When she made a pirouette, he made a pirouette. When she shimmied, he shimmied. When she realized that Kamut Hari was responding, Farrah continued to create more dance moves to the rhythm of her seashells. She performed moves from primal African dance to hip-hop to popping and he continued to imitate all her leaps and gyrations.

Although this was a wonderful game to Kamut Hari, Farrah understood the gravity of their situation and played the game to gain his confidence. When she thought she had gained his trust, Farrah pretended to be exhausted and he offered her a seat on one of the corals. She signaled the clan to recite the incantation, not to deceive Kamut Hari but so that they would all look like him and would gain his trust.

"From the tip of my hair to the tip of my toe, I look exactly like you," they recited.

He spoke in his language and, with her newly acquired power, she was able to understand and communicate with him. She told him that her people needed the help of some of his hidden sacred candles in order to navigate the deepest darkest abyss of the Sulu Sea. She told him about the sea ogres and their prisoner that the clan felt compelled to rescue. With that, she introduced the clan to him.

Kamut Hari said that he had heard tales of the terrible ogres and although he had never met one, he knew that he did not care to. He was very sympathetic to their cause. Farrah's power of persuasion was hard to resist and she was able to convince him to take them to his cave for the small price of a sand dollar shell.

With the rest of the warriors following, Kamut Hari led Farrah through a narrow passage then rode on a strong current to the east. After a few minutes, they entered into a labyrinth reef. Fortunately, they had Kamut Hari to lead them through the three-dimensional maze. It wound around and stopped at dead ends horizontally and vertically. Without the help of Kamut Hari, they would surely have been lost in the maze forever.

When they emerged from the other end of the complicated labyrinth, they found themselves in a cave that contained a garden of coral, stacks of shells, piles of pearls, and a treasure of coins.

Lighting the cave were thousands of asparagus-shaped coral candles that flickered, gleamed, and emitted a constant glow despite being underwater. These sacred candles were truly magical.

Farrah asked permission for the clan to collect some of the sacred water candles. With Kamut Hari's blessing, each warrior took two of the water candles. They each left him a token of appreciation: a hairpin, a thread from their *patadyong*, or a button.

Kamut Hari led them out of his cave and through the maze back to the sunlit reef. Before they parted ways, Kamut Hari wished them luck in their quest, and like a gentleman, he thanked Farrah for the wonderful dances and said that he truly enjoyed the experience. He said that he would practice the dance moves she had taught him and hoped to dance with her again in the future.

Having accomplished the task of acquiring the sacred candles of Sulu Sea, they said good-bye and DJ led the family back to the gateway to Kamut Hari's reefdom. When they had all exited the gateway, DJ locked it securely with the crystal key, and as the Keeper of the Keys had instructed him, he destroyed the crystal key with one smash of a granite rock. The Malipayon warriors journeyed onward to face their biggest mission.

— 20 —

Rescue from the Beyond

As they had been instructed during preparations for this event, they watched each other's shoulders and learned to communicate through their minds. Beyond the western reaches of the reef, they entered the deepest waters of the Sulu Sea. Soon they came to the mouth of an immense chasm, and as they descended into the deepest darkest realms of the abyss, the pressure of the ocean increased against their bodies, but the magical *patadyong*s protected them and they soon reached their destination—The Beyond.

It was very gloomy, but with the aid of the sacred water candles, the warriors were able to navigate through the murky water. In the somber darkness of the deep Beyond chasm, there seemed to be no signs of life, but they knew better. The cold steel of their weapons gleamed as they reflected the warm glow of the candles. The sacred candlelight was somewhat comforting and they summoned all their courage to brave the unknown.

Suddenly, without warning, a shark emerged out of the darkness and sped past them as though it were terrified of something it had encountered as it strayed a little too far into the dismal deep. This ominous occurrence seemed to be a foreboding sign of impending doom.

The water had the foul rotten-egg odor of sulfur, which most likely seeped from a fissure in the earth's crust. DJ used his power to alter the water's condition to be more favorable, but this allowed their human scent to be more detectable. The presence of the Malipayon warriors alarmed a school of blind black carp. They scattered in different directions to alert the sea ogre colony to the invaders.

DJ recalled the fierce ogres of his visions and shuddered. Touching the Librita in his pocket, he chanted, "Give me courage, give me strength, help me fight this battle and be triumphant in the end." By saying this, he regained his focus.

The seabed was gummy. They had to be careful not to touch the ground until they had planted the sacred candles, otherwise they would be trapped in the goop.

Even with such careful preparations and strategy, the terrible sea ogres were ready and began to surround the intruders. Lola had no choice but to reach into her magical *libon* and take out a five-inch-long golden cross. With DJ, Grandpa, and Hans protecting her, she positioned herself as close to the prison site as possible; then she let the cross fall to the ground and it grew thirty feet high. It had a big eye on each end of the horizontal section that opened and beamed two laser-like spotlights that lit up the area as far as half a mile in diameter.

The MacDonalds found themselves in the midst of a school of giant black carp that attacked and tried to devour them. Alex, Laura, and Hanna fought as hard as they could. Unfortunately, each time they killed one, ten more would appear, and they kept charging. A few of the Malipayon warriors tried to help them. DJ was preoccupied with fighting the ogres a short distance away but sensed his family's difficulty. He instructed them to surround the giant carps and use their talismans to blow them up.

"Ah, why didn't I think of that!" said Alex, shaking his head.

They followed DJ's advice, surrounding the carp, and with simultaneous hand gestures, they blew them up with the help of their talismans. The explosion sent pieces of carp flying through the water, but one survived. Unknown to the others, this lone remaining giant black carp scooped up Hanna in its mouth and swam away.

The warriors fought valiantly and tirelessly as new evil creatures kept attacking. At one point, Alex realized that Hanna was missing.

He and Laura tried to find their daughter, but they were constantly drawn into battle by more evil creatures.

The ogres released the giant octopus and electric eels.

The ogres used coral swords. Their spear-shaped tongues and long tails could inject venom into their enemies. They were enormous, as big as houses and each weighed a few tons so they moved very slowly. They kept coming. DJ and the others battled them bravely.

With the help of a few other warriors, the Schroeders faced the giant octopus. It was a long battle. Every time Fritz and Hans cut off the tentacles of the octopus, they grew back.

Carmelita used her magical *patadyong* to blind the octopus, but it counteracted by shooting its poisonous ink at them. Just in time, they used their talismans to create air bubbles around themselves for protection; however, before Julio was able to create his bubble, the octopus wrapped an arm around him and began to constrict his body. It raised him up and was about to slam him down on a rock below, but Julio was able to employ his talisman to coat his body with grease and he slipped away from his attacker.

As they were all floating in their individual bubbles, Kirsten suggested containing the giant octopus in an air bubble before it could do them harm. With synchronized hand gestures and concentrated thoughts, they created an enormous bubble that encased the giant octopus. Since an octopus breathes water and not air, it met its demise in the air bubble. With the help of the warriors, the Schroeders had defeated the octopus.

The Shammari family (Maya, Amir, their son, Aboud, and daughter, Farrah of Jordan) joined with the Leandros family (Marissa, Adonis, and their daughter, Venus of Greece) to battle the killer electric eels. The families combined their powers to defeat them by swimming in speedy circles and maneuvers around them to confuse them, and when the evil eels tried to electrocute the humans, they zapped each other instead.

Meanwhile, the O'Leary family (Evelyn, Liam, their daughter, Emma, and their two sons, Joshua and Sammi of the United States) joined forces with DJ and the rest of the clan to fight the enormous deadly sea ogres. The battle was long and fierce and they were exhausted. Just when it looked as though they might be defeated, DJ made an unexpected discovery when he grabbed the horn of a flailing ogre to propel himself over its head. He discovered that twisting its horn made the ogre pass out and melt into the goop of the seabed. So they devised a plan of attack whereby two of the warriors would keep an ogre occupied and a third would sneak up behind and twist the horn on top of its head. One after another, the ogres melted into the goop and became part of the seabed until they were all exterminated.

The giant carp that had captured Hanna was taking her to the ogre cave to present her to the ruler of the ogres. Inside its mouth, Hanna was uncomfortable. It was dark and slippery.

"Now this is jungle mouth!" she thought. Keeping her sense of humor was Hanna's way of dealing with this frightening experience and gaining confidence that she could overcome her situation.

The carp tightly tucked her under its tongue to restrict her movement but she kept slipping away in its saliva. She had to think fast. She raised her dagger and struck the carp's tongue with great force. The carp went wild trying to spit Hanna out of its mouth. Although it was only a small cut, the giant fish felt electrifying pain, like a human would with a paper cut. Hanna had a chance to strike again. This time she struck with the full force of her talisman. The laser rays of light from the talisman completely slashed off the carp's mouth. She quickly escaped and sped back to the clan to take her position. It was perfect timing; everyone was about to go and search for her. They were relieved that she was safe.

With no time to waste, the clan gathered to synchronize the planting of the sacred candles that they each carried. On the count of three, they planted the candles.

Magically, the candles grew to the size of highway light poles. The light from the sacred candles shone all around them like broad daylight. Any remaining evil creature that was exposed to the light of the sacred candles melted down and disintegrated.

The warriors stood in amazement as the light of the sacred candles revived the innocent lifeless goop-covered sea creatures that had unwittingly strayed into that dreadful ogre colony. They were in awe as each creature began to come to life, move, and transform to its original beautiful colors. The sea grass sprouted, the water sparkled and the beautiful turquoise and emerald colors returned to the colony. Colorful clown fish jumped with delight. Starfish twinkled. Cheerful seahorses pranced and spun around, elated to escape from the slimy goop.

With the defeat of the ogres accomplished and the battle won, there was little time to celebrate. The fierce battle had taken a long time and the warriors could feel the sands of the hourglass running out. Not only was the prisoner's life in peril but their own lives were threatened as time was swiftly approaching the point of no return. DJ continued to lead the Malipayon warriors on their great mission to save the prisoner. The poor creature was fading quickly, and seemed weaker than the last time they had seen him. They had to move quickly and take him to a safe haven for recovery.

DJ communicated to the clan to surround the prison walls and to focus their energy on the prison structure. They inspected the rock cage to see how best to open it. They discovered that it was very tricky and deceiving because it had four locked doors, but they knew instinctively that only one of them would open to free the prisoner. The other three were false doors designed to destroy anyone who tried to free the prisoner.

Before DJ could use his power to open the cage, he had to make sure to open the right door or else the heavy stone structure could collapse and bury them. He carefully scrutinized each of the four doors. The first of the doors had a snake's head handle. It seemed to be alive and could speak. It tried to convince DJ that it was the right door to unlock, but he was not convinced. He went on to examine the next door. The second door had a carving of a scorpion whose tail moved and threatened to sting him as he approached. DJ knew that the scorpion was a desert creature and did not belong in the sea. He was not fooled. The third door emitted enticing music and was covered with sea blooms. The apparition of a woman's hand beckoned DJ to open the door, but again he was not deceived.

He chose the fourth door. It was made of solid igneous rock. There was nothing special about it—nothing convincing, frightening, or enticing. DJ based his choice on faith, logic, and the knowledge that an easy decision is not always the right decision. When he placed the palm of his hand on the Librita and uttered a magic spell, the igneous rock shook and drifted away. DJ had made the right choice.

The prisoner was very weak and barely breathing. He tried to open his eyes, but there was no other movement from him. No one had ever seen this strange creature except DJ, Hans, and Grandpa.

The last thing to do was to unlock the chains that bound the prisoner's feet and wings. The chains were made of thick sea grass. Without hesitation, Grandpa said his magic words and the sea grass released the prisoner. Then, Grandpa called everyone to encircle the prisoner, and with DJ's incantation, a huge air bubble surrounded them all. The bubble hung suspended for a moment and the brave warriors took one last look at the colony they had freed. Then, with the speed of light, they were teleported back to their crystal cave.

— 21 —

The Proclamation of a Shaman Prince

They looked at the altar, and they witnessed the last grains of sand fall to the bottom of the hourglass. They had returned just in time, only a few seconds from the point of no return. They all breathed a sigh of relief and went straight to work treating the Prisoner. No one, not even Grandpa, knew who he was. They had so many questions that needed answers. What did the prisoner want from the Malipayon clan? Why did he choose this clan? Why was he in the undersea prison? How long had he been there? Who were those monstrous sea ogres? Where had he come from?

A few injured warriors needed to be treated quickly. They were rushed to the twin cave underneath the ceiba tree and were laid to rest on its leaves. Exhausted and weak, the warriors felt the warm teardrops that came from the branches. Some drank the refreshing bittersweet drops. The soothing drink restored their health and healed all their injuries. Above the mountain cave, the canopy of the ceiba tree was crying with joy. Its branches swayed back and forth. An eagle that had been nesting on one of the branches was also screeching and flapping its wings with delight.

In the other cave, Lola and Grandpa were looking after the prisoner. They laid him facing the altar on special material that was soft as silk and white as a pearl. Lola wrapped him with care. The fabric was a special *patadyong*, woven from their ancestors' finest and most powerful materials. When he was settled, they fed him the tears from the ceiba tree. Lola retrieved the red-orange pearl with healing powers that DJ, Hans, and Hanna had been given by Mother Pearl. She placed it on the creature's chest above its heart and held it there with the palm of her hand. It took about sixty seconds to revive him. As his appearance was transformed to its former glory, a powerful glow radiated from his entire body and out of the opening of the cave.

This creature had the head of a fierce-looking eagle with a nape of long brown feathers that formed a shaggy crest. It resembled a lion's mane. His face was dark brown with blue-gray eyes. He had a bluish-gray bill that was somewhat arched. He also had a creamy brown crown. His body had the shape of a tamaraw, a kind of buffalo that was indigenous to the northern part of Luzon, Philippines. He was a little bit smaller than a regular water buffalo. His hair was gray and smooth as silk. The front hooves were pearly white, while the edges of the back two were gold. The feathers on top of his wings were speckled brown but those underneath were pearly white. The hair in his tail was also gray.

Now that the creature was revived, they had to complete their mission to the last detail. The warriors performed the shamanistic rituals for healing his spirit that had been captive for thousands of years at the bottom of the ocean.

Once again, the warriors were gathered. Lola said her spells and the shape of the *magna taberna* transformed from a rectangular slab to a round one. She uttered another incantation and the magical creature was on the center of the altar. They formed a ring around the altar and concentrated their power to form a circle of light to sanitize the area from any unwanted power. Holding hands, they stepped eight steps sideways to the right, stomped, then eight steps sideways to the left, and stomped. The altar began to move counter-clockwise. They were instructed to turn clockwise and to touch the edge of the rock slab with their right thumbs on the count of three. When they touched the slab's edge, it zapped their thumbs like an electrified bee sting. The glow of the table intensified and changed direction to clockwise.

In the glowing light that filled the cave, they could see their names floating. Each warrior that fought for the life of this creature was inducted into the Rays of Bravery and Honor of the Malipayon clan.

They chanted and danced to the beat of drums and gongs. Each warrior transcended the realms of both the natural and supernatural worlds in search of the name of this magical creature. According to the Book of Legends, knowing the sacred name of a magical creature was a key to power. The rock slab stopped moving and the warriors came one by one and whispered to the creature a name that they thought might be his. There was no response. His eyes remained closed. Lola and Grandpa tried to identify him, but they also failed. Some had no clue and did not try at all.

Then DJ stepped forward and whispered, "Magnon." The creature immediately reacted by opening his eyes and looking straight at him. Their eyes locked on each other. There was silence inside the cave. DJ could hear every heartbeat. After what seemed like a lifetime, the creature blinked three times, a sign language that only the two of them could understand. DJ should not yet reveal his name; it would remain secret. As for the others, the knowledge that one of them had succeeded in uncovering the secret satisfied them. In that moment, everyone knelt and proclaimed DJ the new shaman prince. The creature closed his eyes. Tears of joy were flowing down his face. Lola wiped them gently with her handkerchief, then he went back to sleep.

Grandpa asked everyone to move to the other cave. They had to leave Magnon alone inside the cave for three days so that he could recover.

When they had all assembled in the other cave, Grandpa requested that everyone who was willing to pursue the warrior status step to the right side. The McDonalds, the Schroeders, the Khans, and the O'Learys stepped to the right without hesitation. They were followed by the two Martinez families, the Al Shammari family, and the Leandros family. Those remaining decided to decline the warrior status for the time being. They might be willing to join in the future, but the dangers that they had encountered in the other world were too threatening to their young families. The elders understood this; each one would have his own calling. This was only the beginning.

Those who did not accept the warrior status were ushered by one of the warriors to another passage where they slid down a small waterfall to a cleansing pool outside. All of their combat memories and any experiences associated with shamanism were erased and could only be revived upon their return to the secret crystal cave. They could only return by invitation of the guardians of the Malipayon warriors, Lola and Grandpa.

The cleansing pool was big enough to hold twenty people. The pristine water was a refreshing combination of fresh and salt water. Once they were in the pool, their only recollections of the day's events were that they had a good time exploring the island and fun swimming. Six small dinghies and servants were waiting to row them back to the cove and the main house.

Those who had remained in the cave had a discussion of their expectations and commitments. They were the ones who would return to the cave in three days. Lola pulled her handkerchief out of her *libon* and shook it three times. Magically, the cave door opened and they stepped outside. Before they turned around, the cave door had disappeared. They were standing in the middle of a meadow. Lola and Grandpa were picking wild lingonberries native to the Philippines for their grandchildren. The rest of them looked back and paid their respects to the ceiba tree that stood high up in the limestone mountain.

The young children who had been left at the main house were busy playing or just waking from a nap. Lola's kitchen was bustling. Life was back to normal. Dinner was squid adobo and grilled tilapia with bird's nest soup to start.

Hanna glanced at her mother and asked, "Is this for real?"

Before Laura could answer, Lola explained to everyone that bird's nest soup was native to the island and that it was made with an actual bird's nest.

After dinner, the aunts, uncles, and cousins surprised DJ for his birthday. They organized parlor games, a singing contest, a dancing contest, and anything they could come up with that involved a competition. They had a great time. It was the best vacation ever. DJ wished it could last forever. He sat down between his grandparents and put his arms around their shoulders saying, "Thank you both. This has been my best birthday ever."

"We are very proud of you," Grandpa replied.

"You certainly made this clan proud," said Lola.

"Yes, your ancestors are watching over you," added Grandpa.

It was after midnight and Lola and Grandpa wished everyone goodnight. When they came to DJ, they said, "Goodnight, my prince."

He kissed them both on their cheeks and replied, "Goodnight."

After everyone else had gone to bed, DJ, Hans, Aboud, Joshua, Noor, and Sammi were still sitting on the dock. The ocean was calm and the breeze was pleasant. They looked at their surroundings and out over the sea and silently thought about the day's events and the mystery surrounding the prisoner they had rescued. Who were the mysterious invaders that the spider woman had referred to as the Hunters? Did more adventures lie ahead? That was the big question.

Epilogue

Vetus Strata

A Tale of a Kingdom

Inhabitants of all worlds were talking about the triumphant and successful mission of an earthly shaman prince who freed Magnon from the deepest ocean chasm. The news spread quickly across the underworld, netherworld, and afterworld of good and evil spirits. Depending on which side the spirits represented jubilation or trepidation occupied their thoughts and filled their hearts.

Kalaharis, reefdoms, kingdoms, and queendoms of lands and seas gathered their inhabitants to proclaim the same message: "It is a time of triumph and a time of prudence, lest we forget how the conflict began and how it ended." How could they?

About the Author:

Corie Laraya-Coutts (a.k.a Corazon) was born on June 5, 1964, in Norala, South Cotabato, Philippines. She is the eldest of twelve children. Her great, great grandfather was a shaman.

She is an undergraduate in Sociology at Ateneo de Davao University, Philippines. She also received a diploma in Child Psychology from the University of Pennsylvania through their distance education program.

She worked as a nanny and caregiver in Kuwait, Egypt, and Hong Kong before coming to Canada in 1996.

Now an entrepreneur, who loves sports particularly golf, hockey, and softball, she lives with her husband, Rod, in Orton, Ontario, Canada.

About the Co-Author/Illustrator:

Hanne Lore Koehler was born in Aachen, Germany, and raised in Canada by loving parents who nurtured her artistic abilities. She married her childhood sweetheart, Stephan. They have two children and two grandchildren. They now live in Cambridge, Ontario, Canada.

During her artistic career, she has painted a wide variety of subjects: action sports art, children's action portraits, landscapes, still life, wall murals, and more. She has written and illustrated a number of children's, youth, and adult books. To see some of her work, please visit www.koehlerart.com.

Ten percent of the proceeds of this book's revenue will be donated to C. Laraya-Coutts Foundations and Trust to support the following causes.

1. Support the Educational Program for New Immigrants in Canada.
2. Support for the Preservation of the Indigenous Community and its People in Mindanao, Philippines.

LaVergne, TN USA
08 September 2010

196359LV00001B/1/P